PREVAILED UPON TO MARRY

A PRIDE AND PREJUDICE VARIATION

MARY SMYTHE

Quills & Quartos
PUBLISHING

Edited by V Lewis, Becky Sun and Regina McCaughey-Silvia

Cover by Susan Adriani at Cloudcat Design

ISBN 978-1-956613-69-8 (ebook) and 978-1-956613-70-4 (paperback)

To my aunt Edith, who never forgot my birthday. I miss you dearly.

CONTENTS

PROLOGUE

Whenever Elizabeth had previously indulged in girlish fantasies of her wedding day, she crafted a lovely image of it. In her mind, she would be married on a perfect summer's day with a sky so blue as to rival all others before it. The gardens about Longbourn and the wildflowers in the fields would be in full, riotous bloom, and the air would be fragrant with their combined scent. She would be dressed in a cheerful yellow silk gown, perfectly suited to the happiest day of her life. Most importantly, the gentleman awaiting her at the end of the aisle—tall, broad, and darkly handsome—would be one whom she could love and respect in equal measure.

Instead, Elizabeth's wedding day was set against the dreary and windy stage of mid-December, the sky neither blue

1

nor clear. Every tree and flower had withered away to spindly stalks, and all she could smell in the air was the faint whiff of oncoming snow. Even her gown, which she had taken little interest in selecting, was a dull, icy blue that could easily be mistaken for grey in dim light. The greatest tragedy, however, was the bridegroom; he was a man she could neither love nor respect in *any* measure.

Far from being the most joyous event of her life, a felicitous beginning to a blissful future, Elizabeth's wedding seemed destined to signal the end of all her dreams. She was attempting to remain sanguine, but with such a regrettable groom, it was impossible to shake the trepidation in her soul. She shivered in the frigid air of the churchyard but could not yet step inside to face what awaited her at the altar, a life so disappointingly disparate from her expectations as to be painful.

How had it come to this? How had she gone from refusing his ridiculous and presumptuous proposal to being minutes away from binding herself to him forever? No matter how many times she reviewed the matter in her mind, Elizabeth could not see how events might have turned out differently. Her family required the sacrifice, and she was not so selfish as to object under the circumstances; thus, the deal was struck. Elizabeth would marry Mr Collins, saving her mother and sisters from destitution after her father's decease. She would then accompany her new husband back to Kent and help him make arrangements for when...

She choked on the sob that bubbled up into her throat. Today was possibly the last time she would see her father alive. Much as she detested the idea of removing to the Hunsford parsonage with only Mr Collins for company, their return to Longbourn was predicated on Mr Bennet's imminent demise. She hoped, therefore, that they might remain in Kent for some time.

Though Elizabeth had been outwardly accepting of her betrothal, a deeply buried part of her had hoped, these last weeks, that some occurrence might still prevent the marriage. Every scenario seemed increasingly unlikely, but she had indulged in them on her long daily walks, if only to preserve her sanity. She had wished that Mr Collins might be struck ill —not dead, just unwell enough to postpone or possibly call off the wedding—or that he would change his mind and choose Mary, who was not so set against him. Elizabeth had even dreamt that another man, a secret admirer, might arrive on her doorstep and beg to take Mr Collins's place because he simply could not bear to think of her married to another.

For one brief, shining moment, Elizabeth had almost believed that this last flight of fancy had come to pass, but Mr Wickham—

No, she would not dwell on *that* disappointment when she had so many others on her mind. Mr Wickham, whom she once considered so amiable and everything charming, had revealed himself to be a cad, and she would no longer give him any attention. He did not deserve it. At least Mr Collins was not unprincipled, or so she prayed.

And so, Elizabeth steeled herself to face what awaited her within. She should, even now, be reciting her marriage vows to Mr Collins, but moments ago she had broken down upon the threshold of the church. Her father had taken pity on her and ushered everyone else inside, closing the door behind him, to allow Elizabeth time to collect herself. Jane, her sweetest, most loyal sister, had remained and was presently waiting a few yards away, a silent sentinel of commiseration.

Elizabeth gathered up her courage, taking a breath so deep that her entire body shook. She was ready. Or, if not quite ready, resigned. *It is time.*

Just as Elizabeth raised her hand to the door latch, she heard clomping hoofbeats behind her. Glad for another reprieve, however short it must be, she glanced over her shoulder. An elegant black carriage pulled by a team of six came into view round the bend. *It is likely passing through Meryton on its way to a more exciting destination.* She could not help but sigh and wish she were aboard it, going anywhere but Kent.

From within the carriage came a shout and, to Elizabeth's surprise, the equipage halted in the middle of the lane. A moment later, its door flew open and a tall gentleman leapt out with a palpable sense of urgency. She startled—*Mr Darcy!* And, just behind him, Mr Bingley. They both raced towards her, the brisk wind whipping their hair and clothing about. Mr Darcy's hat blew off and tumbled down onto the dusty lane, though he seemed not to notice; his grey eyes, which appeared silver against the contrast of his dark wavy hair, were trained directly on her.

For a brief, fluttering moment, she felt hope ignite in her breast at the sight of Mr Bingley. Perhaps he had come to offer for Jane, and she would not have to marry Mr Collins—but no, it was already too late. The banns had been read, the articles signed, and all the parties collected together to witness a marriage. Even if Mr Bingley proposed to Jane this very moment—indeed, the besotted look on his face suggested he might—Elizabeth's fate was sealed. *At least Jane might be happy.*

It did not take long for the two gentlemen to reach them. Mr Bingley, of course, stood next to Jane, but Mr Darcy was immediately before Elizabeth, looking uncharacteristically dishevelled and undone, yet he did not speak.

"Are you well, sir?" she finally asked as she took in his anxious appearance.

His response was unexpected and not to the point of her enquiry. "Am I too late?"

"I beg your pardon?"

"Am I too late?" He paused to swallow, and then seemed more collected. He was staring at her in that intensely probing way he used to do. "Are you married?"

Elizabeth glanced back at the closed door between herself and the altar. "Not yet. I am about to be, but I needed some air."

"Thank God!" Mr Darcy collapsed to his knees and grasped her hands. There seemed a measure of desperation in his movements that Elizabeth could not wholly account for until he cried, "I heard of your betrothal only yesterday, but I have struggled since and it cannot be in vain. My feelings will not be repressed for the sake of others. You must allow me to tell you before it is too late how ardently I admire and love you. I beg of you, relieve my suffering and agree to marry me in place of your cousin."

Elizabeth's shock was thereby complete. To think that Mr Darcy, haughty and unfeeling as he had seemed only the month previous, was at her feet, *begging* her to overthrow Mr Collins and marry him instead! She had pinned her imagined hopes of a rescue on other scenarios, other gentlemen, only to see it materialise before her in the last man in the world she had ever expected to propose.

But was that the truth? Was Mr Darcy truly the last man in the entire world she could envision as her husband? Mr Collins was uncommonly dull, by turns sycophantic and too sure of himself, and behaved as an overindulged child when he did not get his way, but would she be happier with the aloof master of Pemberley? *Except he is far from aloof at the present.*

Apparently sensing her indecision, Mr Darcy pulled both of her hands to his lips and kissed her gloved fingers with passionate fervency.

"Dearest, loveliest Elizabeth." He raised his face just enough to fix her with his gaze, and Elizabeth flushed at the raw emotion she saw therein. "I cannot bear the thought of you wed to another man, especially one such as Mr Collins. Consent to be my wife, and I shall speak to your father immediately. It is not yet too late for us."

The moment Elizabeth had prayed for was now upon her, and yet she hesitated. Could she replace her spiteful cousin with a man she scarcely knew, yet who declared himself hopelessly in love with her? Conversely, could she bind herself to

Mr Collins and face a life of certain misery? She glanced at Jane. Her dearest sister looked to Mr Darcy, turned back to Elizabeth, and nodded rapidly.

At last, she returned her gaze to Mr Darcy, but was interrupted by the sharp squeal of a door hinge and a voice.

"It is time to begin the—here now, what is all this?"

CHAPTER ONE

Three weeks earlier

Bennet threw down his book with a huff. Such a precious volume would customarily be afforded more respect, but it had utterly failed to distract him from his woes and so he felt not a twinge of guilt to see it flop to the floor. Of course, the tragedies of Sophocles were no balm for the sense of foreboding that weighed upon his mind; he had expected too much from the ancient drama. It was, by far, more palatable to heap the blame upon his reading material, or even parties who were not present, but truthfully Bennet was mired in a disaster of his own making.

He had learnt from the despondent wails of his wife the previous evening that Mr Bingley, in whom they all placed such hopes, had gone away with no intention of ever returning to Hertfordshire again. At first, Bennet had been inclined to believe that Mrs Bennet was exaggerating—it would hardly have been the first time—but the letter Jane received from Mr Bingley's wretched sister confirmed the sorry news: Netherfield was closed up, and the entire party was gone off to London.

In happier times, Bennet would have patted his poor, sweet Jane on the head and reminded her that this was the way of things, that young bucks such as Mr Bingley were rarely serious in their intentions or mindful of the tender hearts they bruised with their fickle lovemaking. He might even have comforted her that, next to being married, a young lady likes to be crossed in love a little now and again. Mr Bingley's defection would have given her something of a distinction amongst her friends, but she would get over him in time to be courted by another beau, one more worthy of her affections. But such consolation would ring hollow if his family were turned out of their home with nowhere to live.

Bennet sighed and removed his spectacles to rub the weariness from his eyes. He had obviously been spending too much time listening to Mrs Bennet's lamentations. If he were to die tonight—and there was no guarantee he would not—his wife and daughters would be better cared for than *that*. His brothers, Philips and Gardiner, would take them in, to be sure, though it would still be a mean existence for ladies with little money and few useful accomplishments. And with such a spendthrift mother…well, it was best to make arrangements for them all before he shuffled off this mortal coil, which the apothecary suspected would occur sooner than anyone had expected.

When Bennet first received this dreaded news from Mr Jones, he had despaired. He would not have the opportunity to vex his wife's nerves for another twenty years, nor would he see each of his girls well disposed of in marriage; his life was all but over. He had not immediately given way to panic, however, because at the time, Mr Bingley's flirtation with Jane had seemed to be headed in the right direction. Mrs Bennet, as well as half the neighbourhood, had been in anticipation of an offer from that quarter. But then Netherfield was closed up, and Bennet's hopes were dashed. Mr Bingley would not be their saviour.

There was one obvious solution to his family's troubles, though Bennet was loath to utilise it. His dullard cousin, who just so happened to be his heir, had hinted that he would look after his unmarried cousins should he be granted one of their hands prior to his inheritance. Collins had already approached and been denied by Elizabeth—sensible girl—but with four other single daughters, perhaps a deal could still be struck for the good of all. Bennet despised the thought that any of his precious children, even the silliest of them, should be tied forever to such a man, but there was nothing else to be done at such short notice; it was this or destitution.

A sharp twinge in Bennet's chest stole his breath for a second, and he rubbed at the spot, little good though that did him. Such pains were becoming alarmingly frequent, lending credence to Mr Jones's diagnosis that his heart was failing. He must take immediate steps to protect his family, as he had failed to do before. Once the pain subsided to a steady but tolerable ache, Bennet levered himself out of his chair and rang the bell for Hill. He might as well speak to Collins directly; delaying would not make the interview any more palatable, and it was not as if he had time to waste.

———— ⚜ ————

COLLINS ENTERED HIS COUSIN'S LIBRARY WITH HIS NOSE HELD high, fully comprehending his own dignity. Stumbling over his own feet perhaps injured this dignity a touch, but he ploughed forwards on the heels of the housekeeper as she led him to her master.

He knew not what Mr Bennet wished to say to him, but he hoped it would be an apology for what had occurred the previous day. He was owed it, for Miss Elizabeth had led him on a merry chase for the greater part of a week, only to thoroughly humiliate him. *Impertinent minx!* Well, her rejection was a blessing in disguise; no doubt Lady Catherine would have disapproved of Miss Elizabeth and her empty flirtations.

"Take a seat," Mr Bennet said, waving to a chair placed before his desk. "I suppose you wish to know why I have called you here."

Collins sniffed. "I assume you wish to make amends for the great offence your daughter afforded me yesterday. While I commend you for extending an olive branch, I must say I think it is my cousin *Elizabeth's* duty to beg my forgiveness. Lady Catherine is a great advocate for young women humbling themselves when warranted, as she told me not long ago when a girl in Hunsford village nearly knocked her down in the street. 'Mr Collins,' she said, 'young ladies will never—'"

"Yes, yes," said Mr Bennet with an impatient flick of his hand, rudely interrupting Collins's recitation of Lady Catherine's advice—advice that would be most beneficial to a gentleman burdened with such a surfeit of daughters. "I am sure whatever your patroness advises is most apt, but that is not what I wished to speak to you about, which is to discuss a possible alliance with one of my other girls. Lizzy might not be amenable to your…um, generous offer, but I am certain another would be gratified by your attentions. Mary, perhaps."

"Miss Mary?" Collins wrinkled his nose. Miss Mary was a good sort of girl, in her way, but so very…plain. She had nothing of her elder sisters' charms, either in body or spirit, and she had once made the lamentable error of correcting his quotation of scripture, apparently under the misconception that she knew more than he. He would be surprised if the Bennets ever managed to marry her off. The notion that she would be an acceptable replacement for Miss Elizabeth was laughable.

Mr Bennet's eyes narrowed. "Yes, Mary. She is a pious young woman who would make any clergyman an excellent wife."

Collins snorted. "I think not."

"Very well, then. Which of my daughters would be your preferred choice?"

Feeling justifiably obstinate, Collins replied, "Miss Elizabeth."

Mr Bennet was silent for a long moment, his brow

furrowed in displeasure. "I think we both know that is impossible."

"Nevertheless," Collins said, affecting nonchalance as he examined his fingernails, "she is my only choice. As she has already rejected me, I believe we are at an impasse. Now, if you will excuse me, I am expected at Lucas Lodge to dine. Miss Lucas particularly wished for my company, you understand, and I am always attentive to the felicity of ladies. I would not wish to disappoint her for the world. She, I believe, would make me an excellent wife."

Even if she was as plain as—perhaps even plainer than—Miss Mary, Charlotte Lucas at least showed the good sense to encourage his attentions rather than spurn them, as Miss Elizabeth had done. Added to this, her father was knighted and would elevate Collins's own status. Lady Catherine would almost certainly approve—or so he hoped. He moved to rise from his chair.

"Sit down," Mr Bennet commanded. "I still have three other daughters to choose from. Surely one of them must suit your fancy."

Collins felt his hackles rise at his cousin's rudeness. "I am afraid not." Even the hand of his ethereal cousin Jane was no reparation for the injury done to his consequence. He wanted no more to do with any of them.

"What if Lizzy could be made to accept you?"

Dismissal of Mr Bennet's suggestion dissolved on Collins's tongue. He had, at first, merely used his feigned preference for Miss Elizabeth as a way to put an end to his cousin's pretensions of fobbing off a less worthy daughter on him as a bride. But if she could, indeed, be brought to heel… His interest was definitely piqued.

"I thought you did not support my suit."

A look crossed Mr Bennet's face that suggested he was about to become ill. "I have reconsidered."

"And if Miss Elizabeth still objects to my offer?"

"I am prepared to exercise my authority over her. Although, I must ask, why would you wish for a bride who has already rejected your suit?"

Collins straightened his waistcoat before replying. "Because I…that is…she is my choice, and I shall not change my mind."

What else could he say? That he lusted after her despite her wrongheaded rejection? That he wished to see her brought low and forced to bow down before him? That despite Miss Lucas's good sense to admire him, he longed to break the vivacious Elizabeth Bennet and reform her into the perfect docile wife? He could not admit as such to her father.

Mr Bennet, much to Collins' surprise, did not enquire further. "If I were to approve of the union, would I have your solemn vow that my wife and other daughters would be well cared for after my demise? More to the point, would you be willing to sign marriage articles to that effect?"

Though the notion of being responsible for the two youngest girls was not at all palatable to Collins, he supposed that they could be improved by a hand firmer than what they had become accustomed to in this household. Mrs Bennet already showed good sense in agreeing with much of what he said, and Misses Jane and Mary were similarly malleable.

Further, there was an excellent chance one or more of them would be married off before he was forced to take up their care.

"I would," Collins responded at length.

"Good, good." Mr Bennet still eyed him with suspicion, yet said nothing of it. "I must insist that the marriage take place soon. Before Christmas."

Collins started. He had anticipated a longer engagement in order to seek Lady Catherine's guidance in readying his parsonage for his bride. "Before Christmas?"

"Indeed. You might wonder at my haste, but I assure you that it is necessary for all parties that it should be so. I am not long for this world, you see. 'Tis my heart."

Collins knew that he should feel sorrowful at this news, but instead he was filled with glee. So *this* was why Longbourn's master had so suddenly changed his tune! It had not occurred to him before, but Mr Bennet's hasty turnaround smacked of desperation. Of course he would want to put his affairs in order, lest he leave his wife and children destitute; Collins honoured him for coming to his senses before it was too late. And he was the happy man who would benefit the most from this alteration in circumstances. Suppressing the grin that threatened to spread across his face, Collins affected an air of deep consolation.

"I am most grieved to hear it, sir. Your family will, naturally, feel your loss most acutely, but I can promise you that they are safe in my hands."

Mr Bennet responded to this great condescension with naught but a grunt. Collins was too exultant at his good fortune to be much offended, however. That supercilious Miss Elizabeth consigned to be his wife after all. Longbourn in his possession far sooner than expected. And, most importantly, Lady Catherine's advice to him fulfilled to the letter. All he had left to wish for was an heir of his own, and that matter he would be pleased to undertake once they were properly married—it was his duty, after all, and would hardly be an onerous burden.

He must write to Lady Catherine immediately and request an extension of his stay at Longbourn—oh, and send his regrets to Lucas Lodge; it seemed Miss Lucas was to be disappointed after all.

CHAPTER TWO

"Miss Lizzy, you are wanted in your father's library."

Elizabeth paused in shedding her gloves. Mr Bennet did not often invite her into his private sanctum. She was welcome there, provided she did not disturb his reading, but to be actually called upon to visit him was a rarity. She disposed of her gloves, bonnet, and pelisse in Hill's waiting arms, tiptoed past the breakfast parlour where she could hear her mother's hysterical voice, and knocked lightly upon the library door.

"Come."

She entered but immediately halted upon encountering the further surprise of Mr Collins's presence. She had not seen the clergyman since rejecting his suit the day before, and did not especially wish to endure his petulant and censorious company with any frequency going forth. Yet, there he was, seated in

Mr Bennet's library like he belonged there. *Not just yet, you awful man.*

Endeavouring to ignore her odious cousin, Elizabeth turned to where her father reclined in his customary position behind the desk. "You asked for me, Papa?"

"Indeed." Mr Bennet's chair squeaked as he straightened and waved her closer. "I have some news to share."

Elizabeth sat next to Mr Collins, who seemed yet more pleased with himself than he had from several feet away. She did not like to think what might have made him so suddenly cheerful. Her father, though not often inclined to fidget, moved about in his seat. He then fiddled with his spectacles, readjusting them upon the slope of his prominent nose, and cleared his throat.

"I suppose I shall just come out and say it. Lizzy, my dear, I am afraid that I must rescind my decision from yesterday and insist upon your marrying Mr Collins."

Glancing at her cousin, Elizabeth checked her laugh. Really, it was too cruel to tease the clergyman to his face as Mr Bennet so often did to his wife. No doubt Mr Collins would appreciate it as little as did Mrs Bennet. "Do be serious, Papa. It is not kind to jest in such a fashion."

"I am afraid I am quite serious."

Elizabeth considered her father more earnestly. The grim set of his mouth and the deep furrow of his brow suggested that this was indeed no joking matter. With growing alarm, Elizabeth exclaimed, "No!"

Mr Bennet again squirmed in his seat and would not meet her gaze. "It cannot be helped, I am afraid."

"How *could* you?"

"Dearest Cousin Elizabeth," Mr Collins interrupted. He seemed either unconscious of or unconcerned by her ire, if his superior manner was anything to go by. The leering quality of his roving eyes and the smug tilt of his mouth further added to her disquiet. "I know that your feminine modesty led you astray when I first asked for your hand, but with your honoured father's blessing, you must see that it is time to put any...unwillingness aside and bow to the inevitable, especially with your family's impending change in circumstances."

Elizabeth glanced at her father, who looked yet more agitated.

"And when that melancholy event takes place," Mr Collins continued, "which we all hope will not be for many months yet, though of course we cannot speculate on the Almighty's plan, you can take comfort in the fact that you, your mother, and sisters will be well cared for under this roof, rendering the loss as small as possible."

The world seemed to cave in upon Elizabeth as the horrifying purport of Mr Collins' speech became clear. Of a sudden, she found she could not get enough air into her lungs and that her heart was thudding at an unsteady, fevered pace. With a trembling voice, Elizabeth managed to utter, "Papa, what is he saying?"

Mr Bennet took a deep breath and released it, rubbing his chest all the while. "I am dying, my Lizzy."

Now that Elizabeth observed her father more closely, she could see the signs of illness upon his features. He looked unusually tired for a man who was accustomed to staying up late with his books, and there was an unnatural, almost waxy pallor to his skin, which she had not noticed before. Preferring indoor pursuits, he was never as tanned as Elizabeth, but his complexion he had always been flush with vigour. Even the creases on his face appeared deeper, as if whatever was ailing him had sapped away a decade of his life.

Elizabeth jumped at the touch of cold, spindly fingers upon the back of her hand. She whipped about to find Mr Collins leaning towards her, his face drawn in a detestable mockery of sympathy, eyes glittering with unwholesome glee. "I know this must come as a shock to you, but rest assured that none of you need fear the future. Once we are wed—"

Rising from her chair so rapidly that it toppled, Elizabeth looked back and forth between the two men as her disbelief gave way to horrified comprehension. Her father was dying, and his last wish was for her to marry his heir. To what circle of hell had she descended?

"No, it cannot be true. It cannot!" She clasped a hand over her mouth, feeling ill herself.

Mr Collins reached for her again. She dodged the attempt and his expression crumpled in disapproval. "Now, Cousin—"

"Leave us, Collins."

Mr Collins turned to Mr Bennet, perplexed and churlish. "I beg your pardon?"

"I require time alone with my daughter to explain some things. Do not fear that our agreement will alter."

Mr Collins gave Mr Bennet a surly look, stood in preparation to protest, but ultimately relented. He raked Elizabeth with another triumphant leer and pivoted towards the door. "As you wish. In any case, I have a letter to write."

After the door closed behind him, Elizabeth and her father continued in uncomfortable silence for several minutes. Mr Bennet stared at his hands as if he knew not what to say, now that the moment was upon him. Elizabeth waited, her breathing quick and ragged, for the explanation he had promised.

At length, Mr Bennet looked up at her with burdened eyes and said, "I am so sorry, my dear girl. So very sorry."

———————— ❧✕❧ ————————

JANE FOUGHT NOT TO WEEP AS SHE TOOK HER PLACE AT THE dinner table. Tears had been threatening to spill ever since she received Miss Bingley's note earlier that day. A reprieve from Mrs Bennet's prattle about Mr Bingley would have been most welcome, yet on and on her mother continued, complaining between bites of how ill the Netherfield party had used them.

Jane preferred not to consider it in those terms. Certainly her feelings were hurt, but it was all her own doing. Unless Miss Bingley was deceived herself, which was unlikely, Mr Bingley was already attached elsewhere, and Jane had been deluding herself all along. *How stupid I feel. A man such as Mr Bingley, who could marry anyone, would never—*

The clearing of someone's throat drew her from her thoughts.

"I have an announcement," Mr Bennet said, pausing to glance at each of them in turn.

Mrs Bennet, at the far end of the table, sniffed and glared at her second daughter. "Unless that *unfeeling girl* has come to her senses and accepted Mr Collins, I do not wish to hear it."

Poor Lizzy! Jane offered her a smile of commiseration. Elizabeth, however, would not meet her eye. Jane's brow wrinkled with concern as she noted a certain redness round her sister's eyes and a ghostly pallor to her skin.

"As a matter of fact," continued Mr Bennet, "that is exactly the case. Lizzy has agreed to marry my cousin after all. They will be wed before Christmas."

Jane again looked to Elizabeth, but her sister, with head downcast, said nothing to refute Mr Bennet's claim. This, if nothing else, declared it to be true.

Lydia snorted. "La! What a fine joke. As if Lizzy would change her mind about *that*."

Mr Collins fixed his youngest cousin with a gimlet eye. "I assure you that your father speaks in all sincerity. Miss Elizabeth has agreed to make me the happiest of men."

His speech was interrupted by the joyous felicitations of Mrs Bennet, who praised Elizabeth to the skies for coming to her senses and Mr Collins for having chosen a proper, amiable wife. Lydia and Kitty giggled. Mary pontificated about honouring one's father and mother. Throughout, Jane continued to stare at Elizabeth, willing her to look up and reassure her that all was well. Elizabeth did not oblige.

Mr Bennet recalled their attention by tapping his knife against his glass. "I also regret to inform you that, according to

Mr Jones, there is some trouble with my heart. I know not how long I have left, but you should all prepare yourselves. He expects that I shall not live many months longer."

The deathly silence that descended over the dinner table rang louder than the cacophony of voices that had filled the room just moments before. Mrs Bennet, usually a tempest of nervous laments at the slightest hint of misfortune, was struck dumb. Kitty and Lydia's giggling ceased abruptly. Mary, typically the most stoic member of the family, cupped her hands over her mouth as tears welled in her eyes. Jane simply went still as a heavy numbness overtook her; she hardly knew what to feel.

Elizabeth and Mr Collins appeared to be the only ones unsurprised by her father's announcement, leading Jane to the only possible conclusion: her sister was marrying to save them from losing their home. What else could have compelled her to change her mind about a man she proclaimed ridiculous in every respect? Elizabeth was sacrificing herself to save her family.

Bringing her handkerchief to her trembling lips, Mrs Bennet murmured, "Oh, my dear Mr Bennet..." This piteous whisper broke the spell of silence. Lydia and Kitty wailed and clung to one another. Mary buried her face in her hands and shook with sobs.

Jane remained stupefied, capable only of darting incredulous glances between her father and sister. As the veracity of the situation took hold, the crushing numbness made way for overpowering grief. "Lizzy, no!" she cried above the din, the exclamation surprising even herself.

Elizabeth flinched but otherwise showed no reaction.

Mrs Bennet, uncharacteristically the first to recover her composure, cleared her throat and commanded in a strained voice, "Hush, Jane. Lizzy is doing what she must."

"Indeed, though the news of your father's illness is regrettable," Mr Collins said, nodding solemnly, "you must commend your sister for being so strong at this difficult time. Let us not forget that she will be mistress of this household ere long."

Oh, what a cruel thing to say! Jane could not help but notice the gleam in Mr Collins's eyes. Was he gloating? Surely she was misreading his reaction, as no one with any human feeling could derive pleasure from the impending death of another. Across the table, Elizabeth sat motionless, her jaw tight and her eyes practically glowing with anger. Jane bit her lip to stifle its trembling.

"And when that day comes," her cousin continued, "she will have run of the household. With my oversight, of course. There will need to be some changes, beginning with much stricter economy. When the mourning period has passed, we shall continue to curb many of our social obligations. Why, my youngest cousins are too young to be—"

"Mr Collins," Mr Bennet interrupted testily, "I would thank you to remember that I am not dead yet and remain head of this household until I take my final breath. In the meantime, kindly refrain from rearranging the furniture or withholding pin money."

Mr Collins's visage flushed, and he fell silent for the rest of the dismal meal.

Immediately afterwards, Mr Bennet announced his intention to retire—no great surprise given the precarious state of his health, though Jane wished he might stay with them for a short period. Who knew how much longer they would have the privilege?

Elizabeth took her father's arm as he made for the door. "Allow me to assist you."

Mr Bennet huffed. "I am not an invalid yet. I can climb the stairs on my own."

"I am for bed myself, so it is no trouble."

Jane leapt up from her seat and claimed her father's other arm. "As am I."

Mr Bennet did not argue further, and the three of them made for the stairs. After leaving him to the care of his manservant, Jane followed Elizabeth to their shared bedchamber. They spoke not a word as they prepared themselves for the night, though Jane longed to broach the subject of Mr Bennet's imminent demise, Elizabeth's marriage to Mr Collins, and how in the world they were to overcome so much heartache.

Her sister slipped between the covers without saying goodnight, blew out the candle with a harsh puff of air, and rolled over. Jane was not duped by this pretence of repose. If Elizabeth's trembling shoulders had not given away her upset, her muffled sniffles would have ably performed the office. "Lizzy—"

"I do not wish to speak of it."

Jane's heart clenched at the sound of tears in her sister's voice. She wished to do something—anything—to alleviate

Elizabeth's anguish. "Perhaps...perhaps marriage to Mr Collins will not be as bad as you fear."

Elizabeth's body went rigid.

"He is a respectable man—and family, besides. It says much about his character that he is willing to allow us all to remain at Longbourn after Papa..." Jane choked on her words; she could not yet speak of *that* subject. "It is a kindness that he is not obliged to provide, and we must all be grateful to him. Truly, I think you might be happy with him one day."

Elizabeth gave a harsh snort and turned towards Jane. "I am in no mood to be reminded of Mr Collins' so-called *virtues* after having been bartered to him like a mare at auction." Fury punctuated her every syllable. "I shall make the best of my situation—I have no choice, apparently—but for the present I reserve the right to remain bitter at what has been taken from me, and I beg you to respect that." She rolled back to the wall and said not another word.

In the dark, Jane pondered what she could do. She could not cure her father. She could not sever the entail or improve Mr Collins. She could not entice Mr Bingley to return. She could not even console her dearest sister in her time of great distress. Overwhelmed by her own impotence, Jane buried her face in her pillow and cried herself to sleep.

CHAPTER THREE

Elizabeth's boots scuffed against the ground as she trudged towards Meryton. Ahead of her, Lydia and Kitty clung to one another, heads bent together, as they giggled over which officers they expected to meet there and which was the most handsome. The chatter was irritating —Elizabeth had minimal interest in officers, handsome or not —but their silliness was worth bearing, just to be away from Longbourn and her loathsome betrothed.

Indeed, she was using every pretext available to escape Mr Collins's company while she still could. In less than a fortnight, she would be tied to him forever and subject to his whims; no longer would she be able to scamper off on long walks whenever she liked, nor permitted to while away her leisure hours with a book. Mr Collins had already made perfectly clear that he would not indulge subject matter that had no practical value to a female, and that she would have other duties to attend to in the parsonage and at Lady Catherine's behest. Thus, Elizabeth allowed herself as much enjoyment as possible before her wedding day, and today her aim was to visit the book shop and peruse soon-to-be forbidden volumes.

If only I did not have to marry him!

But it was all settled. The announcement had been made to the neighbourhood, the first banns had been read, and the date was set. To renege now was unthinkable, and doing so would mean her family's certain ejection from Longbourn as soon as her father died.

Elizabeth staggered to a stop in the middle of the lane. The pain of knowing the limits of Mr Bennet's time on earth was so sharp as to render her motionless. The searing sting passed slowly, dragging across her raw nerves like burlap over a new burn. It was nigh on intolerable, especially when she considered that were he hale, her father would never have asked this sacrifice of her.

The rest of her family had no such misgivings. Her mother was triumphant that one of her daughters would be married and that they would continue to have a roof over their heads when Mr Bennet dropped dead. Mary praised Elizabeth for honouring her father and mother, while Kitty and Lydia teased her most cruelly by pretending to make way for her as mistress. Only Jane was truly sympathetic, yet her kind-hearted sister was maddeningly determined to think well of Mr Collins, going so far as to state that Elizabeth might even be happy with him one day. *As if any self-respecting woman could be happy with such a loathsome toad!* But Elizabeth had neither the energy nor the heart to argue with her, so they no longer spoke on the topic at all.

In her woebegone state, Elizabeth had thrown herself upon the compassion of Charlotte Lucas last week, but her good friend only patted her on the shoulder and told her to be grateful.

"Grateful?"

"Why, yes. Grateful. Not only will you be married, but you are the saviour of your entire family. I am sorry to hear about your father's illness, yet aside from that the news is all good. You will have your own home and be of service to your mother and sisters. Many others would trade places with you in a trice. You are fortunate, considering the situation."

She had not seen Charlotte since, save at church the previous Sunday. On that day, Elizabeth studiously avoided her friend's seeking eye, in no state of mind to accept congratulations after the reading of the first banns.

There is nothing for it, Elizabeth thought as she compelled her feet back into motion. She must marry Mr Collins and try to be thankful that her mother and sisters would be provided for. It helped no one if she allowed her resentments to fester.

She acknowledged Kitty's beckoning wave from across the street but shook her head in response. Instead, she indicated the book shop with a nod in that direction and stepped inside.

"Miss Bennet, how lovely to see you this fine morning," said a voice that did not belong to the shopkeeper. "It has been some time since I have had the incomparable pleasure of your company."

Elizabeth jumped, but once her eyes adjusted to the glare

of sunlight filtering through the window behind the figure, she recognised the handsome visage. "Mr Wickham!"

He drew closer, beaming as brightly as a sunny day in June. "Forgive me, I did not mean to startle you."

"There is nothing to forgive, sir. I was not attending to my surroundings." Elizabeth shook her head and pressed a hand to the place where her fluttering heart still raced within her chest. Mr Wickham was as attractive as ever with his warm dark eyes, lustrous blond hair, and charming smile of perfectly straight, white teeth.

Now, had I been required to marry Mr Wickham…

She felt a pang of disappointment that their friendship could never become more. Mr Wickham was the epitome of everything she had ever wanted in a suitor: kind, affable, witty. Handsome, too, which a young man ought to be if he could possibly arrange it. Given the flattering amount of attention he paid her, Elizabeth was reasonably certain that he held her in some esteem. She might have come to love him, if afforded the chance, but she had been robbed of the opportunity. At least memories of the few weeks in his company would sustain her in the difficult years ahead.

He tossed a searching glance over his shoulder, then leant in close and whispered, "I admit that I am pleased for the opportunity to speak with you privately."

In spite of her better judgment and character, Elizabeth felt her hopes rise. Would he declare himself? Her father would never approve—due to that horrid Mr Darcy's meddling, Mr Wickham was next to penniless. Even if she were willing to accept such penury on her own behalf, neither she nor her father could consign her mother and sisters to it. If he were somehow in love with her enough to propose, it would have to be a clandestine arrangement. Would Mr Wickham beg her to come away with him? No, he had far too much honour to make such a suggestion, but...what if—

No, I cannot. Not with her family's reputation and her father's health at stake. It would be better if she could prevent Mr Wickham from declaring himself. Bowing her head, she said, "I...I think I know what you will ask."

"You do?" His ever-present smile hitched up on one side, transforming it into something more reminiscent of a smirk. "I will own that I am surprised, but cannot deny that this makes what I have to suggest easier. It is far preferable to be open about such things."

Elizabeth dragged in a deep breath. "I am sorry to occasion you any pain, but I am afraid that what you wish for is impossible. I...I cannot abandon my mother and sisters to the mercies of Mr Collins. I wish it were otherwise, but..." She stopped as feelings of regret over what might have been engulfed her.

When she raised her head, she found Mr Wickham's smirk still firmly in place. The twinkle in his eye even suggested that he was amused.

"You misunderstand me," he said after a moment. "I was not proposing that you abandon anyone. They need never find out."

Elizabeth frowned in confusion. "Oh?"

"I had something else in mind, something for you to

remember me by once you are married." His eyebrows rose suggestively.

Elizabeth was not especially missish, but she felt her face flood with heat as Mr Wickham's meaning became clear. It was an insulting offer, one that not only offended her morals but also her good sense. How could he think it of her, much less ask so boldly for her feminine favours?

"I can see that you are not yet convinced," he said, stroking a finger down her cheek, "but there is very little risk to what I am proposing. It could easily be arranged. I might meet you out on one of your walks, for instance, or you could sneak into the town if you must have a bed to lie upon. And any potential...*consequences* to our rendezvous could easily be attributed to your husband, should it come to that. I can promise that the experience will be memorable."

Elizabeth's astonishment was beyond expression at first, but it quickly gave way to anger. Swatting Mr Wickham's errant hand away from her face, she glared at him. "And here I was concerned over sparing your feelings, knowing that I must reject you. Of course, that was before I realised you would be offering me something less honourable than marriage."

"Marriage?" Mr Wickham scoffed, his amusement abating somewhat at her tone. "You cannot be serious. I only thought to offer you a bit of passion. You cannot expect to experience it with a man such as Mr Collins."

"And this is what you think of me? That I would compromise every better feeling, every virtue, for a fleeting moment of 'passion'? I have never been so insulted in my entire life! In a way, I feel I must thank you. I shall now go into my marriage knowing that, for all his faults, Mr Collins is at least a more honourable man than *you* have proved yourself to be."

Mr Wickham's face coloured, and his expression lost every trace of teasing insouciance. "I would not be so high and mighty, were I you. You are fortunate that even a man such as Mr Collins is willing to have you, given the smallness of your portion. You have nothing but your charms to recommend you, and no man would take you on so little."

Elizabeth longed to wipe the arrogant expression from his face with some choice words of her own, but her throat constricted, and she was rendered uncharacteristically mute in spite of his provocation. All she could do was to hold her head up high and exit the shop without so much as a backwards glance.

CHAPTER FOUR

T hough Darcy abhorred the idea of an outing, he could no longer tolerate the ennui that had beset him since returning from Hertfordshire. He much preferred to retreat to his study and distract himself with correspondence and ledgers, but he had already completed what little work there was to be done. He was too agitated to settle down with a book, and spending time with his sister meant concerned glances and well-intentioned enquiries into his health, which set him further on edge. And so, Darcy was off to his club.

Eschewing the carriage, he walked through the frigid streets of London, hoping the bracing temperatures would give him something to think of other than that which he so studiously avoided. It was to no avail, however, and his mind wandered back to that which had dominated his thoughts for weeks: Miss Elizabeth Bennet.

Darcy could not fathom why an insignificant country miss beguiled him so, but so it was. He was enamoured of her fine eyes, ready wit, and playful disposition. Never had another woman drawn him in so completely nor made him long to make her an offer. Had she a fortune of her own, or at least a better pedigree, no doubt Darcy would be preparing for his wedding even now. Alas, such was not the case. Elizabeth was everything he had not realised he wished for in a wife, but she was not the sort of lady he should consider as the mistress of Pemberley.

Rationality notwithstanding, he ached daily to return to her and pursue her hand. He would not, could not, yet was miserable with missing her. Darcy did not often dwell on that which he could not have, but he had never before sacrificed so much happiness as when he quitted Netherfield Park with Bingley's sisters, all for the sake of removing himself and his friend from the temptation of marrying for love without prudence.

However, Bingley would not have married for love; his affection would not have been reciprocated. Darcy had no doubt that Jane Bennet would have accepted an offer had Bingley made one, but their match would not have been as satisfying as his own. Elizabeth was warm, open, and affectionate, while her elder sister tended more towards serenity. Not a flaw per se, but Darcy saw no sign that Jane Bennet's heart had been touched, and he could not stand by and allow his friend to throw himself away upon a penniless woman who did not even care for him; Bingley would suffer terribly from such a mistake. And so, it could not be helped: Darcy must stay away from Elizabeth lest he give in to the passion that tormented him, and Bingley must be redirected to a woman more worthy of his devotion.

Upon arriving at his club, Darcy was surprised to spot Bingley across the room, listlessly indulging in a glass of brandy by the fire. His friend was a great favourite amongst the other patrons at White's. It was not unusual for Darcy to wade through a crowd of raucous men and find him at the centre, having instigated the merriment with some joke or a friendly wager. Today, however, he sat pointedly alone. Darcy sympathised with the look of utter dejection on Bingley's countenance. And since misery does, indeed, love company, he turned in his friend's direction.

"Darcy! What do you do here?"

Slumping into the armchair across from Bingley, Darcy replied, "The same as you, I expect. It is far too dreary to remain at home."

"And we all know what an awful object you are with nothing to do on a Sunday evening."

"Quite, although now is Saturday afternoon."

Conversation halted when the waiter arrived. Darcy ordered a brandy to match Bingley's, and they fell into morose silence.

After sitting in the same sullen attitude for several moments, Bingley said, "I might return to Netherfield after the Christmas season."

Darcy ceased swirling his drink. "Are you certain that is advisable?"

"Perhaps not." Bingley shrugged, his gaze cast to the blazing fire beside them. "But I think I shall, all the same."

"You know my opinion on this subject—and your sisters think the same."

"I know, but…perhaps you are wrong. You did not know Miss Bennet as well as I did, and…and I should like to learn the truth for myself."

Darcy sighed and set his glass upon the table next to him. "If you return, you will undoubtedly find yourself obliged to marry, regardless of her feelings. The neighbourhood will expect it. But even if she does care for you as you do her, if she is not as mercenary as I fear, you would still be tied to a barely respectable family. It is not worth the risk."

"Perhaps not for you, but then *you* are not in love."

Bingley's words, spoken more with despondency than ire, nevertheless wounded Darcy. Little did his friend know that he *was* in love, and that it was an equally hopeless cause. As Darcy could not craft any retort that would not reveal his feelings for Elizabeth, he instead changed the subject. "Come, let us not dwell on such maudlin thoughts. Can I interest you in a game of cards?"

After whiling away a number of hours together with cards, billiards, and as much distracting conversation as they could tolerate, Bingley invited Darcy to return with him to the Hursts' town house to dine. Darcy declined, citing the short notice, but ultimately relented for the morrow. He was not looking forward to another Sunday of restless tedium, in any case.

Darcy arrived punctually at the Hursts' town house the following evening, somewhat regretting having accepted Bingley's invitation. A few hours in the company of his friend's disagreeable sisters would do nothing to improve his dark mood. If anything, they would likely worsen it. However, he would be unjustifiably rude to beg off, and so bear up he must.

He rapped the knocker thrice and was admitted by the butler, to whom he was just handing over his greatcoat when Bingley appeared in the vestibule and warmly welcomed him.

"Come. Dinner should be announced soon. I believe my sisters await us in the drawing room."

As they approached, Darcy detected the high-pitched tittering of laughter and suppressed another reflexive urge to flee back to the safety of his own home. *At least I can make my excuses and depart after dinner.* How glad he was that they were no longer sleeping under the same roof at Netherfield.

"And to think I almost gave up *dear Jane's* correspondence," came Miss Bingley's voice from the other side of the door. "I believe I shall keep it up a while longer. Perhaps she will tell us all about the wedding! Would that not be delightful?"

Giggles again erupted, and Bingley came to a sudden stop. Darcy grimaced and halted as well. How he pitied poor Bingley! If it were not bad enough that he was still very much in love with a woman who did not return his feelings, he now had the pain of learning of her imminent marriage, coming mere weeks after his hopes had been dashed. Jane Bennet did not merit an ounce of Bingley's fidelity.

Before Darcy could launch into any speech that might comfort his friend, Bingley rushed forward and burst into the drawing room, surprising his sisters with his sudden entrance.

"What wedding?" he demanded.

Darcy followed him into the room, ready to lend his support, and drew the attention of Miss Bingley. The change in her countenance was instantaneous; she withdrew her irritated glare from her brother and fixed Darcy with an expression she must have believed to be coquettish and alluring. She rose, curtseyed, and fluttered her lashes at him. "Mr Darcy, how pleased I am to see you! It really has been far too long. Why, not since just after we returned to London—"

"*What* wedding, Caroline?" Bingley interrupted, his countenance pale and strained.

Miss Bingley clenched her jaw and breathed in deeply, apparently gathering her patience. Strangely, she spoke to Darcy instead of her brother. "Miss Eliza Bennet is engaged to be married."

The effect of this pronouncement on Darcy was immediate. His vision blurred and he felt weak. His Elizabeth, his beloved, was engaged? It must be a scandalous falsehood! *She could not...would not...*

It then occurred to Darcy in a flash of horror that her engagement might well be some form of retribution against him. Though she had defended Wickham at the Netherfield ball, Darcy had not thought Elizabeth in any true danger from the blackguard at the time. But had he sensed something of Darcy's feelings and targeted Elizabeth? She could be in danger! If not bodily, then her reputation, for Wickham would never actually marry for any sum less than ten thousand pounds.

"Miss Elizabeth?" Darcy barely recognised the raspy croak of his own voice. "Who is she marrying? Tell me it is not Mr Wickham."

"No," replied Miss Bingley, her tone disinterested but her glittering eyes quite the opposite. "Her cousin, Mr Collins."

"Mr Collins!" *Lady Catherine's idiot parson?* Who was also heir to Longbourn, he recalled a moment later. "When?"

"On the morrow. I shall include your congratulations in my response to Miss Bennet, if you like."

Darcy clutched the back of the nearest chair as the floor seemed to sway under his feet. Had he received this news after dinner, he might have cast up his accounts, but his churning stomach was blessedly empty. Regardless, he could not possibly consider eating now.

"Excuse me, I…I am suddenly unwell." He felt feverish as he staggered from the drawing room and made his way back towards the front door. Elizabeth, engaged to that oaf Collins and set to be married the next day! The very thought sickened him.

It was not as though Darcy believed Elizabeth would remain unmarried forever, but he had not expected her to switch her allegiance to another so soon, nor had he antici-pated that her groom would be so completely unworthy of her.

Mr Collins should never dare raise his eyes to Elizabeth, much less take her as his wife. And yet, according to information from her own sister, that was to be her destiny. *What is this madness?*

It had not escaped Darcy's attention at the Netherfield ball that Mr Collins evinced intentions towards Elizabeth, but he had assumed she would never entertain the thought of a union with such a man. Was this his own doing? Had he wounded her heart so deeply that she was content to accept the first proposal to come her way? If he had believed his own misery difficult enough to bear, Darcy must now live with the knowledge that, through his own despicable pride, he had driven the only woman he had ever loved into the arms of his aunt's toadying parson.

Lady Catherine! If Mr Collins by himself was not bad enough, Elizabeth would be forced to endure the never-ending meddling of his tiresome aunt. Not even Elizabeth could bear such interference cheerfully for long; eventually, she would be worn down, and that tantalising sparkle Darcy so adored would be snuffed out. Worse, every time he paid a visit to Rosings Park, he would see Elizabeth as Mrs Collins, surrounded by her poultry and unruly children. *It is not to be borne!*

Darcy halted as a new thought occurred to him. It did not *have* to be borne; he could do something to avert this travesty. Elizabeth was not married yet, merely at the precipice of the altar. If he made haste to Hertfordshire and flung himself at her feet, begged her forgiveness for so callously casting her aside, he could change both their prospects.

It was not too late for him to take Mr Collins's place as Elizabeth's groom, not for a man of his consequence. Another gentleman might be rebuffed, but Fitzwilliam Darcy of Pemberley would undoubtedly be an enticing prize for the comparatively impoverished Bennets. All he needed was to secure Elizabeth's co-operation—she would not deny him out of wounded pride, surely—and speak to her father; then the deed was as good as done.

Bingley dove into Darcy's field of vision, looking understandably concerned. "Darcy, what is the matter? Did Caroline somehow offend you again? I shall speak to her later. Pray, stay for dinner."

"I am sorry, my friend, but I must leave immediately. There is not a moment to lose." So saying, Darcy resumed his speedy walk towards the front door.

Bingley hurried to keep up. "But why? Where are you going?"

"Hertfordshire."

"Hertfordshire! Why on earth would you go there? Has this something to do with Miss Elizabeth's wedding?"

Suddenly aware that this was a conversation they should not be having in the corridor, where anyone might overhear, Darcy opened the nearest door and peeked inside. Discovering the room to be empty, he hurried in and beckoned Bingley to follow. "I am going to Hertfordshire to beg Miss Elizabeth to marry me instead of Mr Collins. I cannot abide the thought that she should be attached to that...that *boor* instead of me, and I aim to offer myself as an alternative."

Bingley stared at him with wide eyes.

"I know this must seem sudden," Darcy elaborated awkwardly, "but I have felt a deep attachment to her for many weeks now, and I cannot allow her to throw herself away on such a man. Perhaps if he were more worthy, I could bear the disappointment better, but even then…I am sorry to rush off like this, but I must return home immediately to make plans. Pray apologise to your family for me."

As Darcy made to leave, he felt a hand grasp his arm. Bingley was still staring at him as if he could not entirely comprehend what was happening, but he managed to speak. "So, you have been suffering the loss of Miss Elizabeth as I have Miss Bennet? All this time?"

"Yes."

"Why did you not say anything to me?"

"I…It is not the kind of thing I am comfortable speaking of, even with a close friend." And Bingley was perhaps his closest, though his cousin Richard might claim the honour. Either way, Darcy was not inclined to reveal so much of his heart to anyone, save perhaps Elizabeth herself. He would certainly have to do so on the morrow.

Bingley released his hand from Darcy's arm. "Take me with you."

"I beg your pardon?"

"Take me with you. If you are intent on marrying Miss Elizabeth, why should I not declare myself to Miss Bennet?"

"Bingley—"

"No, stop." Bingley held up his hand to stay Darcy's objection. "You have made your concerns perfectly clear, but this is something I must see to myself. Besides, how can I remain here when your plan leaves Miss Bennet vulnerable? Without Miss Elizabeth to marry Mr Collins, her family might well force Miss Bennet to accept him in her sister's stead! Just as you cannot countenance Miss Elizabeth tied to him forever, I cannot bear the thought of my angel in the same position. Have some compassion, Darcy, and let me go with you so that I might prevent it!"

Darcy watched Bingley's hardened expression for any sign of wavering and saw none. The man was intent on saving Miss Bennet, that much was obvious. And his worries were not baseless; it was not outside the realm of possibility that the Bennets would substitute their eldest daughter as Mr Collins's bride once Elizabeth jilted him. Darcy was not convinced that Miss Bennet deserved such consideration, but he would not deny Bingley the chance to save his own love from that fate.

"Very well. I shall return here before daybreak, so be prepared. If you are not ready when I arrive, I shall depart without you."

Bingley's face shone with resolute determination. "I shall be ready."

CHAPTER FIVE

To Darcy's pleasant surprise, Bingley was waiting outside the Hursts' town house, dressed warmly and ready to depart, when he arrived before dawn to collect him. Considering the absence of any hysterical shrieks of outrage, Darcy assumed his friend had not informed his sisters of his impending departure, for which he was grateful; there was no room for impediment with time so short. Once Bingley's trunk was loaded, the carriage set off into the lamplit street.

Later, as they approached Meryton, Darcy reviewed his plan once more. They were heading directly for Longbourn in hopes of catching the Bennets before they left for the church. It was already half past eight, but with luck on his side, he would be able to pull Elizabeth aside, tender his offer, and alter both their destinies for the better. It was his dearest hope that all might be quickly and neatly arranged to everyone's satisfaction—save Mr Collins's, he supposed, though his rival's sentiments were not his concern. Darcy consoled himself that the dullard could not possibly deserve Elizabeth and, really, he was saving them both from the misery of an unequal marriage.

There was something to be said for saving the eldest Miss Bennet from Mr Collins's clutches as well. However Darcy felt about Jane Bennet, she did not deserve such a man as her husband. He retained more than a few concerns regarding her lack of attachment to Bingley, but he accepted that his friend was his own man and must ultimately make these sorts of decisions himself. Knowing how desperate he was to call Elizabeth his own, he could hardly fault Bingley for wishing the same with her sister.

Darcy glanced down at his pocket watch yet again and grimaced. The couple could be standing at the altar that very moment. They must hurry. With a heavy exhalation, he tore his eyes from the timepiece and looked out the window. This road would take them past the church on the way to Longbourn.

When they rounded the bend and said church came into view, Darcy's heart seized with alarm and he lurched forward in his seat.

"Elizabeth!"

Indeed, there she was, standing before the church door. Miss Bennet lingered nearby, but otherwise Elizabeth was alone. Did that bode well for his plans, or ill? Darcy cried out for the coachman to stop, and disengaged the latch with trembling fingers just as the carriage jerked to a standstill. He flung the door open, burst through it as if propelled by a mighty wind, and sprinted towards Elizabeth.

Darcy had prepared a speech about how he desperately wished to marry her despite her unfortunate connexions to trade, how he was ready and willing to put aside any disparities that existed between them to make her his wife. Now that she was before him, her fine eyes regarding him with astonishment, he found himself lacking the wherewithal for such a recitation. Indeed, he struggled to proffer so much as a simple greeting. Bingley seemed in similar straits as he stood next to Miss Bennet.

After a long stretch of overwrought silence, Elizabeth asked with concern evident on her countenance and in her voice, "Are you well, sir?"

Her question forced Darcy's mind back to its regular function. "Am I too late?"

"I beg your pardon?"

"Am I too late?" *Dear God, let it not be too late.* "Are you married?"

"Not yet. I am about to be, but I needed some air."

Darcy felt much of the fear and apprehension of the past four-and-twenty hours dissipate at her answer. Elizabeth was not yet married, so he still had a chance to make her his own. In his exquisite relief, he dropped to his knees and exclaimed, "Thank God! I heard of your betrothal only yesterday, but I have struggled since and it cannot be in vain. My feelings will not be repressed for the sake of others. You must allow me to tell you before it is too late how ardently I admire and love you. I beg of you, relieve my suffering and agree to marry me in place of your cousin."

If Elizabeth had seemed surprised at his arrival—and why should she not be after the way he had abandoned her?—it was nothing to what her face was now expressing. Clearly, she had not expected him to return.

He pulled both her hands to his lips and kissed them with all the passion he had suppressed since almost the very beginning of their acquaintance. "Dearest, loveliest Elizabeth," he implored, "I cannot bear the thought of you wed to another man, especially one such as Mr Collins. Consent to be my wife, and I shall speak to your father immediately. It is not yet too late for us."

Her eyes strayed to where her eldest sister stood observing them. Miss Bennet's face showed more emotion than Darcy had ever witnessed on her as she nodded with rapidity, apparently bestowing her blessing upon them. He was grateful and, for the first time, at peace with the idea of her becoming Mrs Bingley.

Elizabeth swallowed visibly and returned her eyes to Darcy. He was encouraged to see some of their former sparkle returned but remained anxious over her hesitation. Would she choose to oblige her family and marry Mr Collins after all? As crushing as such a result would be, Darcy could understand the desire to avoid scandal, even if the price would be a lifetime as that dolt's companion. How he hoped that she would follow her heart and disregard the pitfalls, as he had.

After a long stretch of silence, Elizabeth breathed in deeply and made as if to speak. Before she could utter so much as a single syllable, however, the church door opened behind her and her father stepped out.

"It is time to begin the—here now, what is all this?"

Darcy scrambled to his feet and bowed to Mr Bennet, disliking how awkward and dusty he must seem to the man who held the power to approve or deny his suit. "I have come to ask Miss Elizabeth for her hand in marriage."

Mr Bennet goggled at him. "You have what?"

Darcy bit back his impatience, fully aware that his words and actions were outrageous, and said again, "I wish to marry your daughter, Miss Elizabeth. I was just asking her to become my wife a moment before you appeared."

"You do realise that she is about to marry my cousin?" Mr Bennet sputtered. "He is standing at the altar this moment, awaiting his bride to begin the ceremony."

Glancing at Elizabeth, who continued to stare at him in much the same way as her father, Darcy replied, "I am well aware, and I offer myself as an alternative bridegroom—if she will have me." Not that he had much doubt, but it would not be safe to assume in these unconventional circumstances. "I can procure a licence, and we can marry as soon as you deem acceptable."

Mr Bennet eyed him shrewdly. "And would you be prepared to support my wife and unmarried daughters in the event of my death? Mr Collins will not take kindly to being jilted, and is likely to thrust them all out of Longbourn soon after I take my last breath."

Though Darcy hardly wished for the responsibility of caring for Mrs Bennet and the younger girls, it would be his duty to protect his wife's family; Mr Bennet need not have bothered to ask this of him. "Of course."

Mr Bennet's wary gaze remained fixed upon Darcy as he asked, "Well, Lizzy? It is up to you. Would you prefer my witless cousin or Mr Darcy?"

Darcy felt a lump form in his stomach as Elizabeth's eyes flicked back and forth between him and her father. She could not possibly prefer Collins to him, could she? No one of any sense would take Mr Collins, who was as ridiculous as he was inconsequential, over the master of Pemberley. Yet her hesitation weighed heavily on him. How he longed to convince her with a kiss, but with so many witnesses, such a risk would likely be rewarded ill. However, he could—and did—reach out and graze the back of her hand with his fingers.

Elizabeth startled and looked down to the point of contact between them, gazing uncomprehendingly at their mingled fingers. She then set her mouth into a determined line, took his hand, and squeezed it. Darcy's anxiety immediately dissolved into nothing.

"I choose Mr Darcy, Papa."

Mr Bennet drew closer and bent towards Elizabeth, his voice a low murmur. "Are you certain, my child?"

Elizabeth swallowed and raised her chin. "Yes, sir."

Mr Bennet peered at her pensively for several tense heartbeats before he let out a deep sigh and closed his eyes. "Excellent, then we are all in accord." He opened the church door with one hand as he waved his daughters and their beaux through with the other. "Come now, step lively. There is no time like the present to make a few announcements."

CHAPTER SIX

When Darcy stated his intentions, Bennet's initial emotion was shock, quickly followed by a powerful sense of relief. It had never been his desire to parcel his favourite off to Collins, but there had seemed no way round the unpalatable obligation at the time. Had he even the slightest inkling of Darcy's interest in Elizabeth prior to this day, he might have considered other avenues, but, then again, the man had hied off to London on his friend's coattails. How was Bennet to know?

In retrospect, he *had* seen some signs. Bennet thought little enough of it at the time, but at Lucas Lodge in October and at every other social occasion thereafter, Elizabeth seemed to have a gravitational pull on Darcy's gaze. *And I believed him looking to find a blemish! My spectacles must not be doing their office.* Further, now that he considered the matter more closely, the taciturn gentleman had danced with Elizabeth, and *only* Elizabeth, at the Bingleys' ball, thus gravely disappointing Netherfield's husband-hunting hostess and many a matchmaking mama.

How had he missed it? The family's salvation had been right in front of his nose, and he possessed not the powers of observation to discern it. Not that it signified any longer. Darcy was here now, and matters were resolved to everyone's satisfaction. *Well, almost everyone's.*

Upon crossing the threshold of Meryton's church, Bennet paused to survey those who had come to witness Elizabeth marry Collins. The guest list had been restricted to family only, as she had not wished for a fuss—no doubt feeling that there was little reason to celebrate her union. But those who loved her best, or at least expected the most from her, were present.

Bennet's three youngest daughters were at the front, each of them exhibiting signs of impatience. Mrs Bennet's brother Gardiner and his wife sat at the far end of the family pew, speaking quietly to one another and darting concerned glances at the pontificating groom. Bennet knew that Gardiner had strong opinions about what Elizabeth was being forced to do; he had said as much last evening in the privacy of Bennet's library. Undoubtedly, Mrs Gardiner was of the same mind, if the cool formality he had received from her since their arrival was any indication. They, at least, would be elated to hear of this new turn of events.

And what would Mrs Bennet think? Bennet hoped that her caterwauling would be more joyous than dismayed when he announced Elizabeth's decision. Any gossip the family might endure, once it was known that Elizabeth had left a man at the altar, would be trampled under her new consequence as Mrs Darcy. Her soon-to-be husband had ten thousand a year and relations in the peerage; what was Collins to all that? Such should be enough to soothe Mrs Bennet's nerves.

Standing in front of the altar and pontificating to the long-suffering Reverend Brown, Collins was speaking of his parsonage's numerous merits. The boorish imbecile seemed excessively pleased with himself as he waited for Elizabeth and boasted of his good fortune.

Well, that feeling will fade soon enough. A portion of Bennet's good humour returned and made itself known in the form of a sardonic smile.

He glanced back at his second daughter, who clung limply to her new betrothed's arm. She appeared pale, perhaps a bit ill. But then again, she had just narrowly escaped from the maws of a miserable fate. Any lady might look a little peaky in similar circumstances. Still, Bennet could not easily forget her previous opinion of Darcy, and fretted that her wan appearance bespoke more than momentary bewilderment.

Bennet had never believed a word of the nonsense spread about by Mr Wickham that Darcy had denied him a living; a naïve young woman might be bamboozled, but Bennet was immune to the lieutenant's pretty charms. No doubt Darcy had his flaws, but Bennet hoped they were only of the common variety and nothing especially dastardly. The gentleman was obviously well educated and could string together an entire sentence without once mentioning Lady Catherine. Moreover, he showed the fine taste of preferring Elizabeth to every other lady, not to mention tremendous honour and affection in swooping in to marry her. Yes, Darcy was preferable to his idiot cousin in every respect, and for the first time in many months, Bennet's heart was at ease.

"Mr Bennet!" his wife called out at the top of her voice. "Who is that with you? Is that...Mr Darcy? What is he doing here?"

And here I wondered how I might introduce the subject.

Bennet cleared his throat. "You are uncannily observant today, madam. Mr Darcy is, indeed, here—and for a particular purpose. To marry our Lizzy, as a matter of fact. As she has accepted him, I have granted them my permission to wed." He hoped that Mr Bingley might soon ask for Jane as well, but it was perhaps best to take one betrothal at a time, lest his wife actually expire from too much happiness. It would not do to leave the girls entirely without parents.

The silence that followed Bennet's proclamation was every bit as ringing as his wife's cry had been. Save for the recently reunited couples at his back, he was regarded by all present with uncomprehending bewilderment. At first.

Collins, with his usual measure of unwarranted confidence, was the first to speak. "Very amusing, Cousin. I can see where your lovely daughter has inherited her wit, however misplaced it is. A gentleman as exalted as Mr Darcy of Pemberley would never condescend to—forgive me—marry someone of such low birth."

Mrs Bennet gasped and clasped a hand to her bosom. "Well, I never!"

Rankled, Bennet glared at his cousin. "As I stated," he said slowly so that the dullard would have no room for misapprehension, "Mr Darcy here has travelled from London to ask for Lizzy's hand and, as she has accepted his offer, she will be marrying him instead. I am sorry for any inconvenience, sir, but so it is."

Collins' self-assured grin wavered like a candle flame caught in a passing breeze, but he quickly recovered himself. "It cannot be. No, you are sporting with me. Really, Cousin, a good joke is fine now and then, but in circumstances such as these—"

"It is entirely true," came a low voice from behind Bennet.

He turned with the rest of his family to regard Darcy, who stood with the regal bearing and confidence of one who is rarely, if ever, gainsaid.

Darcy pulled Elizabeth closer to his side and observed those present with cool hauteur. "I have asked Miss Elizabeth to be my wife, and she has graciously accepted. As soon as it can be arranged, we shall be wed."

Elizabeth gazed up at her new betrothed with apparent wonder, flushed a deep red, then looked away again. Bennet could not be sure, but he thought she might be overwhelmed by Darcy's determination to marry her. With the considerable surprise of his declaration and the unusual circumstances of his proposal, Bennet could not blame her.

Collins's cheeks puffed out and his skin splotched most alarmingly. "But-but you cannot! Lady Catherine would not approve!"

Darcy looked unconcerned. "I am my own man and make

my own decisions. I shall not be turned from marrying Miss Elizabeth on my aunt's say so."

"But Lady Catherine is almost the nearest relation you have in the world, sir! The daughter of an earl! Whose opinion could possibly be afforded more weight?"

"Mine," Bennet said. With Elizabeth safe from Collins's clutches, some of his natural inclination to quip had returned. "As Lizzy's father, I have the very great responsibility of accepting or rejecting any suitor on her behalf. If Mr Darcy has extended her an offer and Lizzy has accepted it, why may not I allow them to marry?"

"B-because honour, decorum, prudence, nay, interest forbid it," cried Collins, looking increasingly undone. "Cousin Elizabeth cannot expect to be noticed by Mr Darcy's family or friends if she wilfully acts against the inclination of them all. She will be censured, slighted, and despised by everyone connected with him. Their alliance will be a disgrace, her name never mentioned by any of them!"

Elizabeth looked to Darcy with alarm writ across her face, but his attention was elsewhere.

"Preposterous!" Darcy exclaimed. "If—and I cannot believe that such would be the case—the indignation of my family were excited by my marrying Miss Elizabeth, it would not give me a moment's concern. Even then, the world in general would have too much sense to join in the scorn."

Bingley joined his voice to the cause with a loud "Hear, hear!" It seemed his friends, at least, would not be so ridiculous as to abandon him for marrying a country lass.

"As it is," Darcy continued, "the choice of whom to wed is

mine and mine alone. Anyone who disapproves, regardless of their affiliation with me, is of no concern to me."

So saying, he turned away from the still sputtering Collins and gazed down at Elizabeth with undisguised adoration. She returned this intensity with a trembling smile and a faint glow that seemed, to Bennet, a promising start to their new life together.

The matter put to rest, the party began chattering happily amongst themselves. Kitty and Lydia were giddy with the romance of it all and how envious the rest of the neighbourhood would be. Mary preached decorum while being utterly ignored. The Gardiners sat with their heads bent together, talking quietly, and even from a distance Bennet could see how much more relaxed they were. *Good. Perhaps I might avoid further chastisement from that quarter.* The reverend and the Philipses stood just beyond Collins, watching the scene unfold with a small measure of concern but much bemusement.

Mrs Bennet was the loudest of them all, crowing about how much pin money and how many gowns, jewels, and carriages Elizabeth would have as Mrs Darcy. She also debated aloud as to whether she should reside primarily at her new son's country estate or relocate to London to find husbands for her younger girls. Bennet shook his head at her but shared her relief. When he departed this world, they would be amply provided for. With this, he could be content.

"What about Miss de Bourgh?" This enquiry burst from Collins and drew the notice of everyone within the church walls.

"What about her?" Mrs Bennet scoffed. "If she had expectations of Mr Darcy, I am sorry for her, but that is nothing to *us*."

"She had more than expectations," declared Collins. "Indeed, she has been betrothed to Mr Darcy from infancy. He cannot marry Cousin Elizabeth because he is already promised to *her*!"

—— ⁎⁎⁎ ——

COLLINS FELT AN INORDINATE AMOUNT OF SATISFACTION WHEN Mrs Bennet collapsed into her brother's arms. *That will teach you not to cast me off so easily, you hateful shrew.*

When Mr Darcy first appeared, Collins had been beside himself with pride. To think that the exalted Mr Fitzwilliam Darcy, nephew of Lady Catherine de Bourgh of Rosings Park, condescended to attend his wedding! Of course, that was before he realised the great travesty unfolding before him.

He was disgusted by the way Miss Elizabeth clung to Mr Darcy's arm, acting as though his attentions were her due. Had she no notion of propriety or her lower rank? He could only imagine the arts and allurements that the scheming jezebel had used to draw him in—and all while she was engaged to another! It would serve her and her atrocious family right if he left them to starve. He certainly did not wish for a faithless wife such as she.

But first, he needed to save Mr Darcy from offending his

illustrious aunt. Miss de Bourgh's prior claim *must* come before Cousin Elizabeth's. His announcement to that effect had an immediate result, much to his gratification. In particular, he was pleased to see the fickle woman pale to the colour of overly skimmed milk. Oh yes, let her truly appreciate the trouble that she was in. It was what she deserved, after all.

Mr Brown enquired gravely, "Mr Darcy is already engaged elsewhere?"

"No!" replied Mr Darcy with vehemence. "My aunt claims it to be so, but I have never acknowledged it. It was merely something she and my mother talked of when my cousin and I were babes."

The reverend's eyes darted between Collins and Mr Darcy. "Well, if the gentleman has never—"

"I have seen the contract myself." It was a lie, but Collins comforted himself that it was only a small one, and God would surely forgive him for it. All he need do for the nonce was to prevent Mr Darcy and Cousin Elizabeth from saying their vows until Lady Catherine could be called upon to set everything to rights. She would come to Hertfordshire, praise him for his good sense and quick actions, scold everyone into the correct way of thinking, and all would be as it was before. If the Bennets were very lucky, Collins might even still marry the fair but faithless Miss Elizabeth and spare them the humiliation he was currently experiencing. He was sure he could stamp out any remaining pride and disobedience in his future wife. *With Lady Catherine to strengthen me, I can do all things!*

"You lie!" Mr Darcy snarled. "I swear before God and everyone present that no such document exists."

Mr Brown sighed and cast his eyes heavenward. There was only one thing he could do, however, and Collins knew it. His role as a clergyman was clear.

"I believe you, Mr Darcy, but the objection has already been raised, and I am obligated to investigate Mr Collins's claim. If there is no document, as you assert, then you and Miss Elizabeth are free to marry. But if this document does exist… Well, let us call upon Lady Catherine to either prove or disprove an existing betrothal to Miss de Bourgh, and we can settle the question once and for all."

Mr Darcy continued to argue with Mr Brown, but the parson stood firm. Collins' scheme had worked, Lady Catherine would have her say, and all would be right with the world. He could hardly wait.

CHAPTER SEVEN

Rarely had Darcy felt such an urge towards violence, yet Collins' smug expression made his hand curl into a fist, ready to thrash the sanctimony right out of the man. Claims about a betrothal to Anne, a legal marriage contract—all lies. Not only would Darcy never have signed such a thing, he knew his father had been against the alliance. Wealthy and connected his cousin Anne may be, but hale enough to continue the Darcy line she was not.

Collins, the pompous imbecile, wore a triumphant grin. No doubt he believed that Lady Catherine would settle the matter to his liking, but Darcy was not so weak as to fold to her demands. Admittedly, he had hoped to present his marriage to Elizabeth as a *fait accompli* and thus render ineffectual his aunt's interference, but Darcy was able to withstand any barbs or threats she cast their way. He would not be swayed from his choice.

Mrs Bennet wailed, "We are ruined!"

"Calm yourself, Sister," soothed Mrs Philips. "Even should Mr Darcy prove to be engaged elsewhere, I am certain Mr Collins would still have Lizzy. All will be well."

"No, no, we are ruined forever! Lady Catherine's horrid daughter will steal Mr Darcy, and that evil Mr Collins will turn us out of our home before Mr Bennet is cold in his grave. Mr Bingley will have no choice but to leave us again, and then where will we be? Begging in the streets, I say!"

A fashionable-looking lady gently shushed her. "There now. You will not be forced to beg. You have family to take you in, should the worst happen."

"Indeed," agreed a gentleman of middling age who cradled Mrs Bennet's hand within his own. "No one would allow you or the girls to suffer. I would not listen to that oaf in any case. Mr Collins is a pitiful, spiteful man with more words than sense. If Mr Darcy says he is not engaged to Miss de Bourgh, then I daresay he is not, and this will all be cleared up. By this time next week, he will be leading Lizzy to the altar, mark my words."

Collins, who apparently cared nothing for his own self-preservation amidst so many who clearly detested him, scoffed. "I have it on the authority of Lady Catherine de Bourgh herself that Mr Darcy is engaged to her daughter. Cousin Elizabeth may have distracted him with her feminine wiles, which she wields indiscriminately against many gentlemen, including myself, but—"

Darcy lurched forward with a balled fist to defend Elizabeth's honour, but she clutched at his arm and said, "Do not rise to his bait. He is unworthy of it."

As Darcy struggled to control his temper, the gentleman seated next to Mrs Bennet said, "Hold your tongue between your teeth if you cannot speak sensibly, Mr Collins! There is not a person here who takes kindly to your abusive speech against my niece."

"I second that recommendation," Darcy said. "Be silent lest you wish to find yourself called to the field of honour. I would take great pleasure in teaching you a few manners, but you are not worth the trouble." He nodded to his beloved, and a relieved smile was his reward. He then glanced at Mr Bennet, seated towards the back of the church, his forehead resting against his palm and looking very much defeated. *Why does he not come to his daughter's defence?* Darcy's jaw clenched.

Collins sputtered and staggered backwards. "Threats are entirely uncalled for, sir!"

"Then keep such slanderous nonsense to yourself."

"Hear, hear." Elizabeth's uncle sneered at Collins before returning to console Mrs Bennet, although his ministrations did little to moderate her nervous complaints.

"And now both Mr Darcy and Mr Collins will be killed in a duel, and no one will be left to marry Lizzy! Oh, I feel the faintness coming upon me!"

While Miss Mary administered her mother's smelling salts, Darcy redirected his gaze to Elizabeth, still clinging to his arm, and discovered her to be ashen and shaking. His expression softened into one meant to convey reassurance, but she would not look at him. A sharp sensation of dismay stabbed him in the gut. "Are you well, dearest?"

Elizabeth swallowed and bowed her head so that the brim of her bonnet covered her face. "I…I do not know. This is all happening so fast."

Darcy pulled Elizabeth into the vestibule, where they could have some semblance of privacy. "You are not having second thoughts, are you? I swear to you that I am not, nor have I ever been, engaged to Anne or any other woman. You must believe me."

"I do. However, I fear…" Elizabeth took a deep, shuddering breath. "Perhaps it would be easiest to let Mr Collins and your aunt have their way and be done with it. I would not wish for you to regret your choice."

"Never say such a thing!" Darcy declared. He placed his hands upon Elizabeth's shoulders and bent down, forcing her to meet his eyes. Within hers, he found a tangle of emotions amidst a sheen of tears. "You are worth all this and more. I care not for Lady Catherine's opinion, and I care even less for that clod Collins's. Do not forsake me to appease others, I beg you."

Elizabeth blinked rapidly, and a single tear ran down her cheek.

Darcy wiped it away with the pad of his thumb. "Please."

She glanced past him into the sanctuary and bit her lip. "My father…"

Darcy followed her gaze and discovered Mr Bennet in the same position as before, looking pitiable and impotent. Could this man stand up against Lady Catherine? As Elizabeth had not yet attained her majority, Mr Bennet's consent was required. It was clear he did not wish his daughter to marry a buffoon, but Mr Bennet's reputation was that of an indolent man accustomed to capitulating to the loudest demands—his wife and youngest daughters' wild and uncouth ways were a testament to that inclination. And Lady Catherine was not known to brook disappointment. Feeling a surge of panic, Darcy instinctively pulled Elizabeth closer.

"Go," said a quiet yet insistent voice.

He turned round to find Jane Bennet a few feet away with an expression of resolve firm upon her countenance. Bingley stood just behind her with similar purpose in his mien.

Darcy stared at her. "I beg your pardon?"

"Go," Miss Bennet repeated, this time looking to her sister. "Elope. Make for Scotland and marry over the anvil."

"Jane?" Elizabeth whispered in bewilderment.

Miss Bennet offered Elizabeth her hand. "I know it sounds mad, but I believe this is your best chance at happiness. I know not what sort of contract Lady Catherine has, or whether our father will change his mind again, but no one can prevent your marriage if you escape now."

To say Darcy was nonplussed would be a vast understatement. Placid, demure Jane Bennet was advocating elopement, something so beyond the scope of propriety as to be downright disgraceful, thus tainting not only the couple but also everyone connected to them. Darcy doubted that Bingley would forsake Miss Bennet, but how would the scandal affect the prospects of Elizabeth's other sisters? Of Georgiana?

"Out of the question," Darcy finally managed to say. "I cannot—I will not elope. It is not right!"

"You have already come this far, sir, and interrupted the legal marriage of two people whilst a question hangs over your own eligibility to wed. Will you stop there, or will you do what you came here to do and rescue my sister from a wretched fate?"

Miss Bennet was persuasive, Darcy had to admit.

Elizabeth bit her lower lip. "But how can I, Jane? What of Papa? What of our sisters?"

"Oh, Lizzy." Miss Bennet blinked rapidly. "You have been so brave lately, so selfless in accepting Mr Collins for all our sakes. It is now time to do something for yourself. If you truly cannot countenance a life spent as Mr Collins's wife, I implore you to take this opportunity and abscond with Mr Darcy. You have a chance for happiness with him that you cannot expect here. Do not worry about Papa, or me, or anyone else. Go and do not look back."

Darcy smiled in admiration of the lady. Miss Bennet's manner might be soft, but her spine was made of iron.

Bingley added his voice to the debate. "Miss Bennet is right—this is your best chance, Darcy. I know you are considering all the possible consequences, but I pray you to forget them and go. You have the resources, there is nothing stopping you."

Oh, how Darcy was tempted! But did he dare? One glance at Elizabeth's face, which now brimmed with newfound hope, decided him in a moment. Of course he dared; he would risk this and so much more to save her—save them both—from a lifetime of misery and regret.

He held out his hand. "Come, Elizabeth. My carriage waits outside."

Elizabeth's eyes flicked one final time to her father before she straightened. She embraced her sister, smiled at Bingley, and slipped her hand into Darcy's. "To Scotland."

———— ⚜ ————

AM I OUT OF MY SENSES TO BE ELOPING WITH THIS MAN?

Perhaps. However, Elizabeth's courage had risen and she would not be deterred. Somehow, eloping with this enigmatic gentleman seemed a more sensible choice than being shackled to Mr Collins, and so they raced out of the church as if the hounds of hell were upon their heels.

"Carter!" Mr Darcy shouted, rousing the attention of his coachman. "We must away, and quickly!" Without waiting for the footman's assistance, Mr Darcy wrenched the carriage door open, scooped Elizabeth up with one arm, and all but threw her inside. He then planted himself on the bench beside her and slammed the door. Leaning out the window, he barked, "Turn round. We make for the north—to Scotland."

To the coachman's credit, he did not question his master's commands, and the carriage began to move.

Struck by a sudden thought, Elizabeth grabbed hold of Mr

Darcy's arm and exclaimed, "Wait! I have none of my things for a long trip."

"We have not the time for you to pack."

"There is no need. Mr Collins wished to set off for Kent directly after the wedding breakfast, so my trunk is already packed and waiting at Longbourn."

Mr Darcy appeared torn as he glanced at his watch, but he ultimately capitulated. It was but a few minutes later when the carriage halted in Longbourn's drive, and fewer still until the luggage was properly strapped on and they were off.

Elizabeth wished they did not have to pass by the church again, but there were no routes from Longbourn that might avoid it. She sucked in a deep breath and gripped Mr Darcy's hand as they approached. His steady presence was such a comfort to her jangled nerves. Thankfully, nothing appeared amiss as said church came into view. She released her breath and sank back into the leather squabs.

"Stop! *Stop!*"

Elizabeth's spine went rigid at the sound of Mr Collins's frantic voice, and she whipped about to look out the window. Her erstwhile bridegroom was waving from the church door and shouting frantically for the carriage to halt. Just behind him, the rest of her family flooded into the churchyard to add their voices to his. She could not tell whether they were scolding or encouraging her escape, but she assumed it was something of a mix.

His commands unheeded, Mr Collins started to chase after them but fell face-first on the flagstone walk. The last Elizabeth saw of him, her uncle Gardiner and Mr Bingley were holding him down.

"Richly deserved," Mr Darcy muttered.

Elizabeth turned and found his face hovering just over her shoulder. He smirked with evident delight and raised an eyebrow, inviting her to join him in his amusement. Blushing furiously at his nearness, she returned to the window.

As they rounded the bend that would take them away from Meryton, she spotted Jane waving goodbye with joyous enthusiasm. Just beyond her stood Mr Bennet, his expression inscrutable from a distance.

CHAPTER EIGHT

"Off! Get off of me!" cried Collins, flailing his arms against Mr Bingley and Mr Gardiner's hold.

Mr Gardiner stepped back, hands in the air. "Now, now, we only meant to help."

Mr Bingley, likewise, released him and backed away, leaving Collins to struggle to his feet alone. He might have done so with more grace had their so-called assistance not cost him his composure.

"You tripped me!" he cried breathlessly.

Mr Gardiner did not deny it. "Perhaps you ought to be more cautious where you step."

Collins desperately wished to give the tradesman a blistering set-down, but he had not a moment more to lose if he were to catch up with Mr Darcy and Cousin Elizabeth. For Lady Catherine's sake as well as his own, he must put a stop to whatever scheme they had concocted. His patroness would be displeased, to say the least, if he allowed them to escape. Even though he would soon become the master of Longbourn, and thus no longer beholden to his patroness for his living, no good could possibly come from a hostile estrangement with such a revered personage as Lady Catherine de Bourgh. Collins shuddered at the thought.

By the time he managed to right himself, the carriage was gone. A light cloud of dust along the lane was the only sign it had ever been there.

"Curses!"

The couple had snuck off like thieves in the night. The brazenness, the effrontery, the unmitigated gall! To flee in broad daylight with witnesses all about was…it was…she was…

"My brave girl!"

He turned in disgust to Mrs Bennet who was sobbing into her handkerchief, visibly overcome by her own felicity.

"And I thought Lizzy hated Mr Darcy." Miss Lydia giggled like the ill-mannered hoyden that she was. "She was always saying so, was she not, Kitty?"

"I thought it was Mr Darcy who hated Lizzy!" replied her sister. "He called her 'not handsome enough to tempt' him at the assembly, remember?"

"He has obviously changed his mind about her! Why, did you see the way he looked at her? If Mr Wickham ever stared at *me* that way, I would not think twice about running away with—"

"Lydia!" Miss Mary scolded. "Do you not comprehend

what our sister has done? She has tarnished her good name and ours along with it. A woman's reputation is as beautiful as it is brittle, and such a misstep in one sister must be injurious to—"

"Oh, hold your tongue, girl," interrupted Mrs Bennet. "Lizzy has done just as she ought by eloping with a rich man instead of settling for Mr Collins. I might have wished for them to stand up in church where all our friends could see her, but at least she will be married—and to a man worth ten *thousand* a year!"

"But Mama—"

"No, I will hear no more of your strictures, Mary. You would do well to emulate Lizzy's boldness. Perhaps then you might attract a wealthy gentleman of your own."

Seeing that the female faction of Bennets was a lost cause of silliness and immorality, Collins turned to their patriarch. "Cousin, we must make haste and go after them. Lady Catherine will be beside herself if we do not put a stop to this madness!"

Mr Bennet sighed and raised his eyes to the heavens. "I am afraid I cannot oblige you, Mr Collins."

"How do you know for certain that their intent is marriage?" Collins insinuated. "For all we know, Mr Darcy means to set Miss Elizabeth up in London and grant her a carte-blanche." He would not have expected such unprincipled behaviour of Lady Catherine's relation, but then again, he had never imagined that the illustrious Mr Darcy would steal his bride, either.

"You have already been warned to have a care with my

niece's reputation," Mr Gardiner said with a low growl. Both he and Mr Bennet were glaring at him, though Collins did not think he had said anything out of turn.

"I can assure you that Darcy's intentions are entirely honourable," interjected Mr Bingley. "Miss Bennet and I spoke to them before they left, and they are, indeed, headed to Scotland."

"But Mr Darcy is betrothed to his cousin, the fair and noble Miss Anne de Bourgh! He cannot marry Miss Elizabeth when Lady Catherine expects him—"

Mr Bennet raised his hand. "Regardless of what Lady Catherine expects, my daughter and Mr Darcy will be married over the anvil. I have not the resources to intervene, and neither am I in a fit state to do so. You must be content. I shall not go after them."

Collins ceased his objections, too outraged to argue further. He had awoken that morning ready to take his comely cousin to wife—had been upon the precipice of that happy event—but all had gone awry. What was he to do now?

Worse, how was he to tell Lady Catherine?

———— ⊱✕⊰ ————

JANE'S ARM LOWERED SLOWLY BACK DOWN TO HER SIDE, AND she sighed as the carriage bearing Elizabeth and Mr Darcy rounded the bend and disappeared from sight. In the wake of so much excitement, her mind was awhirl with emotion. She was simultaneously relieved that her precious sister need not face a future with a man she could not respect; satisfied that Elizabeth and Mr Darcy had taken her advice to elope; bewildered by the speed with which everything had happened; and, worried about the couple's journey and Elizabeth's ultimate felicity with Mr Darcy.

Despite some unease, Jane believed everything would be well, that Elizabeth had made an excellent match with Mr Darcy who, for all his faults, appeared to love his bride most violently. Did not his willingness to throw aside social convention say it all? Her greatest concern was Elizabeth's ability to be content in her new situation, given her sister's obstinate adherence to her own opinions. If Elizabeth could but overcome her prejudice against Mr Darcy, she might at last allow herself to be happy.

"Miss Bennet?" came Mr Bingley's tremulous call, barely audible over the din about them.

Jane had been expecting him to speak to her since his precipitous arrival, and thus she was able to turn to him with a practised calm that had seen her through many a tribulation. Inside, she trembled. "Yes, Mr Bingley?"

"I..." He was wringing his hands so assiduously that it would be a small miracle if his gloves were not soon ruined.

It would be up to her, it seemed, to initiate a conversation. They were far from alone, but the congregated party was too distracted to pay them much mind. It was as good a time as any to resolve something that had been niggling at her. "May I ask you a question, sir?"

He swallowed and cast his gaze downward. "Anything."

"How did Mr Darcy know to come for Lizzy?"

Some of the tension from Mr Bingley's shoulders released. He was also able to meet her eyes again, albeit tentatively. "From your letter to Caroline. She was telling Louisa of your sister's engagement when Darcy and I happened upon them. I have never seen such a look on my friend's face before; he was ghastly white and visibly disturbed. He left that instant and began preparing for his return to Meryton."

"And you wished to attend him? As a friend?" It was not like Jane to drop such hints, but she could hardly ask Mr Bingley outright if his own return had aught to do with herself.

"Well…" Mr Bingley's gaze again fell to the ground, but he brought his eyes back up to hers almost immediately. "Yes, but that was not the only reason."

Jane's heart stuttered. "Oh?"

"Yes. I had hoped that I might…we might…that is…I know I left somewhat precipitously after the ball, but I had always intended to come back directly to…to continue our acquaintance. Staying away for so long was unforgivable, I know, but—"

Just as Mr Bingley was finally coming to the point, Mr Bennet raised his voice above the cacophony and called every-one's attention. "As there is to be no wedding today, there is little benefit in standing about in this stupid manner when we could all be more comfortable at Longbourn. Let us go and enjoy our breakfast. No reason it should go to waste." So saying, he began the walk towards his estate at a determined pace.

Mr Collins was the first to fall in step with him, and was

soon followed by an incensed-looking Mr Gardiner. The rest straggled along in their wake, giggling and gossiping with loud enthusiasm.

Jane heaved a small sigh and made to join the procession, but halted at a slight tug on her wrist. She looked down to find that Mr Bingley had captured it, and felt warmth wash into her cheeks.

"Another moment, please, Miss Bennet."

"Of course, sir."

Mr Bingley breathed in deeply before he began. "I understand completely if you cannot forgive me for leaving without a word last month, but I do hope that you will consider granting me the very great honour of…becoming my wife."

Jane lifted her eyes to Mr Bingley's countenance, which appeared equal parts earnest and anxious. She swallowed down her own nerves to respond. "May I ask why you did not return?"

"I am embarrassed to say it, but I did not trust your feelings. Darcy and my sisters convinced me…" He shook his head sharply and started again. "No, I shall not place the blame upon them. It was my own cowardice, my own failure to rely upon my better judgment, that caused me to act as I did. I ought to have sought the truth myself, but I allowed others to lead me about by the nose instead. I am heartily ashamed of my conduct and swear to do better in the future, if you can but forgive me and accept my hand."

Jane paused. "But you do love me?" she eventually asked.

Mr Bingley's eyes softened, and he clasped her hand to his

heart, which beat rapidly beneath his fine blue coat. "Very much."

"Then…yes. Yes, I shall marry you." With her acceptance, the past weeks of uncertainty, melancholy, and self-recrimination faded away to be replaced by an effervescent joy Jane had rarely, if ever, experienced. To love and be loved in return— what more could any rational person wish for? "We all make mistakes and—"

Jane was unable to finish her forgiving speech because suddenly Mr Bingley's lips were upon hers, and she forgot what she meant to say.

CHAPTER NINE

Upon returning to Longbourn, Bennet retreated to his library, but the atmosphere there was far from the peace he had hoped for after such a tumultuous morning. Gardiner, Bingley, and Collins had followed him into his inner sanctum, the latter pacing while ranting about Elizabeth's defection—or, more precisely, what Bennet should be doing about it.

"You must go after them!"

Bennet repeated his prior refusal. "You must resign yourself to what is before you. Lizzy and Mr Darcy will be married, and there is nothing any of us can do to prevent it."

"But surely something can be done!" Collins wheedled, his voice pitched high in a petulant whine. "They are not so far gone that we cannot catch up if we leave now."

"Are you witless?" countered Gardiner. "They have a good head start and are likely travelling at great speed. A man such as Mr Darcy can change horses as needed, increasing their chances of evading pursuers. Where we would be required to stop and rest, they might continue on unhindered. No, we have no chance of catching them, none at all. It would be a fool's errand to attempt it."

Bennet wished he could believe his brother was taking his part to preserve him from the strain of Collins's complaints, but he knew this assistance was likely more to facilitate Elizabeth's escape. Gardiner had made it abundantly clear that he resented the decision to promise her to Collins, scolding Bennet harshly for not coming to him instead. Perhaps he should have done so, but he doubted his brother's ability to feed so many additional mouths at his table. He had his own growing family to be concerned with.

Bingley, who was apparently not as meek as Bennet had supposed, lent his support. "I have had it from Darcy himself that the betrothal to his cousin was merely Lady Catherine's wish and nothing more."

Bennet noted that this was the seventh time Bingley had conveyed this same information to Collins. Not that the dullard would accept it. For nigh on two hours, Collins had pressed for something to be done while the other men resisted.

Finally and with much petulance, he accosted them with one final threat. "If you will do nothing to bring your wayward daughter back, then I shall go to Lady Catherine! Her ladyship will know what is to be done, and woe betide anyone who attempts to thwart her."

Bennet, fatigued and irritated, snapped in return, "Go, then, and take word to your beloved patroness. I care not.

However, you may wish to relay your message upon your belly because I expect she will be vexed with *you* above all others."

It was most gratifying when Collins blanched. "What do you mean?"

"Was it not your own betrothed with whom Mr Darcy absconded? Lady Catherine might assume you bear a certain responsibility in these proceedings. But then, you know her best—is she a forgiving soul?"

Collins's mouth flapped open and closed, but it seemed his defence of her ladyship had its limits. He no doubt knew what it was to fear Lady Catherine's wrath.

At length he spoke again, but changed tactics. "If…If you will not go after them yourself, then I insist upon borrowing your carriage to see to the pursuit in your stead."

"I am afraid I cannot allow that," replied Bennet. The pleasure of denying Collins brought a wry smirk to his lips. "Not only is my equipage not in the sort of condition which would allow for long journeys, but the horses are required on the farm. I can send you as far as London, but no farther. You must make your way home from there, as previously arranged, or hire a carriage if you wish to chase after anyone."

"But…but you must allow me to—"

"The answer is still a resounding no."

Collins turned to Gardiner. "Then I must insist upon commandeering *your* carriage, sir. I am sure you can spare it for the sake of righting a tremendous wrong and bringing your niece home."

Gardiner snorted. "I think not. I am of no mind to assist

you, and my family is as much in need of our equipage as Bennet is. I must return to London and my business upon the morrow, and cannot have you gallivanting about the country in my only mode of transportation."

"Mr Bingley?" Collins transferred his imploring expression, which was becoming more impatient by the second, to the final person in the room. "You, as Mr Darcy's friend, know the very great condescension owed to Lady Catherine. Lend me your carriage so that I might give chase and prevent this travesty of a marriage!"

Bingley squirmed at being put on the spot, but shook his head. "I arrived in the same coach that is now taking Darcy and Miss Elizabeth north. Even if I wished to help, I cannot."

"Is that so?" Bennet asked lightly. "In that case, I shall be happy to convey you back to Netherfield at any time convenient."

"I thank you, sir, but I have been invited by Mrs Bennet to dine."

"Very well, I should like to have a word with you regardless. You are most welcome."

"And I, too, would appreciate a private audience with you."

"I need a carriage!" Collins exclaimed, stomping his foot in a remarkable imitation of Lydia.

Restraining the urge to laugh, Bennet replied, "It seems there are no carriages to be had, sir. You might like to check in the village to see if there is one for hire, or perhaps catch the stage going north, but that is the best any of us can do. I shall be happy to convey you to London, as I have already stated, but you must find your own way to Gretna Green."

Collins's eyes narrowed into vengeful slits, and his nostrils flared. "I will not forget this," he promised before spinning on his heel and storming out of the room.

The pall of Collins's threat weighed heavily upon him, but Bennet breathed more easily once his idiot cousin was gone. He rubbed his temple with the tips of his fingers in hopes of assuaging the headache that was building behind his eyes. He could not fault Elizabeth for running from the pompous clod, but he did wish she had shown more compassion for her papa's poor nerves. And Darcy, whom Bennet had previously considered a steady, responsible sort of gentleman, had proved to be as susceptible as any lovesick ninny to romantic impulses.

"What I cannot understand," Bennet complained aloud, "is why they felt the need to elope at all. I had already granted them my permission and, assuming the likelihood that Collins was mistaken about that so-called marriage contract, they needed only to wait. Why do something so reckless?"

"You can hardly blame them, Bennet," Gardiner said with undisguised contempt. "With my sister wailing that the entire family was doomed, Collins threatening to involve Lady Catherine, and you sitting about saying nothing to anyone, I doubt Lizzy and Mr Darcy felt they had much choice. They probably thought you would change your mind."

"I would never! I was more elated than anyone, including Lizzy herself, when Mr Darcy showed up begging for her hand. Collins is a half-wit, but Mr Darcy has at least a chance of deserving her."

"With all due respect, Mr Bennet..." Bingley paused, swallowed visibly, and continued, "It looked very much like you were reconsidering your earlier decision."

"Poppycock!"

Gardiner laughed, though more in disdain than amusement. "He is right, Bennet. You have always surrendered to the loudest complaint. When was the last time you stood resolute against your wife's propensity to overspend? When have you ever taken the trouble to check one of your girls? Lydia, especially, need only stamp her foot to get her way. You detest confrontation and thus give in at the slightest hint of bother to yourself. Had you been more of a father, had you demonstrated more strength of will, you would not have had to barter Lizzy off to your ridiculous cousin, and she would not have, in turn, felt the need to run away with Mr Darcy."

Bennet stared at Gardiner with his mouth agape. He was nearly too surprised to be offended, though of course some indignation was natural. "I say, you give your opinion very decidedly for someone who has never had the burden of an entailed estate."

"I might not be a landowner, but I know what it means to be the head of one's household."

Bennet wished to slash back with his rapier wit but found there was no profit in it. Gardiner was not entirely wrong. Had he not chastised himself these past three weeks for making Elizabeth's sacrifice to Collins necessary? He should have put aside more money. He should have prepared for his family's future. He should have taken the entail more seriously rather than put off thinking of the inevitable.

Reaching for the decanter on the shelf behind him, Bennet said, "I know it is still early, but I could use a nip of brandy. Would either of you like to join me?"

It was agreed all round that a glass would be most welcome, and a toast was lifted in honour of the Scotland-bound couple.

CHAPTER TEN

The butler of Lord and Lady Matlock's London home entered the gold drawing room. "A Mr Collins is here to see you, ma'am."

Lady Catherine de Bourgh peered regally down her nose at the mangled card presented to her. She was far too occupied to attend her sweaty-handed parson. With a flick of the wrist, she dismissed the butler and his salver. "Send him away. I am not at home to him."

"Who is this man?" enquired Lady Matlock. Beside her, Lady Catherine's daughter, Anne, startled awake with a soft grunt.

"Merely my parson from Hunsford," replied Lady Catherine with a dismissiveness that declared the subject closed. She then took a sip from her cup and curled her lip in distaste. Clearly, her sister by marriage had not taken her advice on the best places to purchase tea; this was an inferior blend. Before she could comment on it, however, the butler cleared his throat.

"I beg your pardon, my lady, but Mr Collins says his business is urgent and insists that he must see you immediately. He says it has to do with your nephew Mr Darcy."

The blistering reprimand Lady Catherine intended to unleash on the presumptuous servant faded from her tongue as curiosity grabbed hold of her. What could Collins possibly have to do with Darcy? She was aware that the two had been introduced, per Collins's letters, which were so long and full of details as to inform the reader what he ate at every meal and the hours of his waking and sleeping. But surely there could be no other connexion between them. By Collins's own report, Darcy had left Hertfordshire nearly a month ago, and Lady Catherine would never suspect her nephew of agreeing to correspond with someone so far beneath his notice.

"Very well, show him in."

The butler shifted on his feet. "Mr Collins further stated that his business is of a delicate nature and suggested that privacy would be—"

"Bring him here!" Lady Catherine punctuated her command with a sharp rap of her cane upon the floor. Lady Matlock's placid countenance flinched ever so slightly, but Lady Catherine had no care for the parquet; her sister would do well to hire more obedient servants who would not vex their guests beyond endurance.

The butler scurried from the room at last, and the ladies proclaimed themselves curious as to Mr Collins's purported 'urgent business'.

"What can he mean, coming to me here?" Lady Catherine complained.

"And what is his connexion to Darcy?" Lady Matlock enquired.

Lady Catherine narrowed her eyes at her, suspicious of her interest in that quarter. The mistress of Rosings Park had never wholly forgiven the other lady's attempt at pairing Darcy with her own daughter two years ago, in flagrant disregard of Anne's prior claim. With Frederica safely married elsewhere, however, and no other daughters to settle, it seemed an innocent enough question.

"I can hardly fathom it. They are barely acquainted, and I am certain we have seen him more recently than Collins has; my nephew and niece are here in London, though one would hardly know it. They have not been to visit in over a week! Anne is heartbroken over Darcy's neglect."

Lady Catherine waved her hand vaguely in her daughter's direction. Anne's heartbreak must have been excessively fatiguing, for she had fallen back to sleep in her pile of shawls.

"You know how young men are," Lady Matlock remarked, then took another sip of tea through her smirking lips. "Always busy with this and that. He has promised to be here for Christmas."

"Mr Collins."

The ladies inclined their heads in the direction of the drawing room doors to see the pudgy, sweaty parson hurrying forward, bowing repeatedly and with such fervour as to nearly overset himself a time or two.

"Lady Catherine, I arrived as soon as I could! I have such dreadful news, so dreadful that I detest the necessity of revealing it to you, but there is not a moment to lose! No, we must act at once to prevent a travesty of the worst sort from taking place and ruining, perhaps forever, the happiness of your beloved daughter. Why, I hardly know what to say on the subject other than that I am most heartily ashamed of my relations and their—"

Lady Catherine again rapped her cane upon the floor. "Speak plainly, sir! What is this dreadful news you bring me? Of what are you talking?"

Collins ceased his ridiculous rambling, wrung his hands together, and bounced on his feet; he appeared far more agitated than usual. "Of Mr Darcy and my cousin Elizabeth!" he blurted.

Lady Catherine gritted her teeth; truly, the dolt either gave too much or too little, never quite coming to the point without an inordinate amount of redirection or prodding. "What of them? Is this cousin of yours not the one you married this morning?"

"Yes—well, no—that is, I had intended to marry her this morning, but events transpired—events that were not my fault, I promise—and my betrothed has run off to Scotland with Mr Darcy."

"Is this some kind of horrible joke?" Lady Catherine's voice boomed throughout the room like a peal of thunder. "If so, I am decidedly not amused!"

Collins recoiled several paces, tripped over his own feet, and fell to the floor in a graceless heap. "I-I am not joking! I saw them drive off myself. I swear I did everything I could to stop them. Forgive me!"

"What? You lie!" Lady Catherine leapt to her feet, causing Collins to flinch and retreat further.

"N-no, your ladyship, it is true. My cousin Elizabeth, a jezebel of the first order, has wiles and allurements enough to tempt any man into desiring her. If I had any idea that Mr Darcy had succumbed to her arts whilst in the neighbourhood, I would have alerted you immediately, but I did not know—"

"And you allowed her to use these arts on my nephew, knowing he was destined for Anne?"

"Of course not! I had not the faintest idea of their being attached to one another, I swear it! I had heard that Mr Darcy did not find her handsome—"

"This is how you repay me for all I have done for you? For elevating you to your position, for educating you in the ways of a gentleman, for seeing to your every need? You let your wanton cousin, your *own* betrothed, elope with my daughter's intended? This is how you show your gratitude?"

Lady Catherine unleashed a stream of loud invectives against the cowering parson, who huddled on the floor in a cringing ball, weeping openly. Were she not so preoccupied, she might have thwacked him once or twice with her cane.

Lady Matlock attempted to calm her, encouraging her to lower her voice to avoid the notice of the servants, but Lady Catherine refused to be placated. Anne simply kept her eyes closed, huddled deeper into her shawls, and leant into Mrs Jenkinson's coddling ministrations.

"I declare, what is going on? We could hear shouting all the way from the dining room."

The commanding tones of Lord Matlock suspended Lady Catherine's diatribe. She turned to the door where he and his two sons, Lord Marbury and Colonel Fitzwilliam, were hurrying into the room. Fitzwilliam closed it behind them.

"This *worm*"—Lady Catherine pointed to Collins with her cane and hissed through clenched teeth—"has allowed Darcy to run off with his betrothed, a grasping upstart who obviously saw a better prize and wasted no time in casting the idiot aside!" And on she went, telling the sorry tale to her brother with seething ferocity.

More than once did Lord Matlock insist that she lower her voice, saying, "You would not want the servants to get wind of this, I am sure," and more than once did she forget and begin shouting again.

"Something must be done!" she insisted "Brother, we must go after them at once and put a stop to this shameful affair before it is too late!"

Lord Matlock exchanged looks with his wife, who wrinkled her nose in turn. This silent communication seemed to settle something in his lordship's mind, for he turned to Lady Catherine and replied, "No, I think not. As ashamed as I am of Darcy's behaviour—and truly, he will receive the reprimand of his life the next time I see him—I believe it would only make the gossip worse if we were to give chase. It would be much better to keep this matter as hushed up as possible, perhaps framing it as a private wedding rather than an elopement.

Assuming, of course, that your caterwauling has not alerted everyone in London already."

Lady Catherine was aghast. *Betrayed by my own kin!* "But what of Anne?"

Lord Matlock glanced at his niece and sighed. "I am sorry for Anne, but this disappointment was inevitable. Darcy never would have married her. I wish he had shown her more courtesy than staging an elopement with another, but there is nothing to be done for it. Perhaps now you can focus on finding her a more appropriate husband, as I have been encouraging you to do these last three years at least."

"Yes, indeed," chimed in Lady Matlock with a serene smile. "I know several young gentlemen with titles who would be most happy to make Anne's acquaintance. What they lack in fortune, they make up in consequence, and so an alliance would be most—"

"No! *Anne is engaged to Darcy!*"

Her relations looked decidedly weary. It was her brother who next attempted to cajole her out of her justified fury. "Catherine, be reasonable. Darcy is officially off the marriage mart, and we must think of Anne's future."

"How can you say such things?" Lady Catherine was appalled. "You would allow Darcy to bring some country nobody, a grasping upstart, into the family? And after such atrocious behaviour from the pair of them? I demand that you go after them!"

"No," Lord Matlock stated calmly.

Lady Catherine then turned to her two nephews and insisted that they oblige her in their father's stead.

Marbury straightened his cuffs, appearing indifferent. "Not I. I cannot say that I commend Darcy on his choice but I have no intention of dashing off here, there, and yon on a pointless errand. Let him make a fool of himself if he will, but I shall not join him in the endeavour."

"Fitzwilliam?" Lady Catherine implored of her younger nephew, but found no ally there, either.

"I dearly wish to oblige you in all things, Aunt," he replied with smirking insouciance, "but I am afraid that I agree with my parents and brother in this rare instance. Darcy is free to make his own choices, and I am not inclined to stand in his way. Besides, I cannot simply abandon my duties to king and country on a whim. Do consider the silver lining in this dark cloud, however. Now you will not have to suffer the presence of—what did you call her? Oh, yes—a grasping upstart in your parish. She will now be placed far away from you at Pemberley."

The half-hearted scolding Fitzwilliam's mother gave him for this impertinent speech was drowned out by Lady Catherine's howl of outrage. "Traitors, the entire lot of you! Well, if you will not bestir yourselves to preserve the family honour, I shall do it myself!"

"Catherine, you cannot be serious—"

Lady Catherine ignored her brother's entreaty and stalked from the room, Collins scuttling after the hem of her skirts.

CHAPTER ELEVEN

The fugitives had travelled at breakneck speeds for hours and were well out of reach of any possible pursuers. They were as physically comfortable as two people who were absconding together could be: fine leather benches, hot bricks at their feet, rugs tucked round them to ward off the December chill. Elizabeth had never been in an equipage so lavishly upholstered in her life. However, there was such an air of awkwardness therein that it rendered every luxury moot.

Not a word had been spoken since Mr Darcy urged the driver's speedy departure from Meryton, and Elizabeth, despite her gregarious disposition, could think of nothing to say. It was a rattling, nervous sort of silence, the kind that seemed to place an embargo upon every subject, both significant and benign.

Mr Darcy seemed to feel it as keenly as did she. His gaze

found hers often, but it would skitter away the next moment as if fearful of being caught. His fingers tapped incessantly against the leather seat, and he shifted about frequently, causing the upholstery to squeak and his blankets to rustle. It was clear to Elizabeth that he was uneasy, now that they were alone and the excitement of their escapade had waned. Or perhaps he was regretful; it was difficult to say with any certainty.

Elizabeth's own feelings were in flux, a natural consequence of the improbable situation in which she found herself. On the one hand, she was relieved to be away from Mr Collins and the fate she had only barely escaped. On the other, it was extremely strange to be in a carriage bound for Gretna Green with a gentleman she had once considered the worst possible candidate for a husband—at least until she had met Mr Collins.

Indeed, in the weeks since their acquaintance began, Elizabeth had not thought kindly of Mr Darcy, and now she was eloping with him, of all things. Had anyone asked her, before he prostrated himself at her feet and begged her to marry him, she could never have predicted how their association would turn out. Even in her wildest fantasies of rescue, Mr Darcy never played a role; that honour had been Mr Wickham's until he insulted her. After that, she had stopped imagining any sort of deliverance.

Considering subsequent events, it seemed her opinion must face a revolution. She had believed Mr Darcy looking to find fault, yet apparently his gaze held nothing but admiration —even ardent love. She had been wholly mistaken about his disapproval! After all, did not actions speak louder than words? Mr Darcy's willingness to risk his good name with an elopement absolutely shouted better feelings than she had ever supposed of him before and, thus, invalidated all her former opinions of the gentleman.

Elizabeth prided herself on her ability to sketch characters, yet she had misread Mr Darcy, utterly and completely. She had certainly never thought him capable of so much passion prior to this morning; he had always been aloof and austere during his stay at Netherfield. His hauteur had given her the impression that he looked upon her with disdain—much the way he looked upon the rest of her acquaintances—but evidently it had merely been masking his ardour. The notion of him pining for her in such a way made her stomach flutter.

Other than Mr Darcy's poor first impression, one based at least partially on her own flawed perceptions, Elizabeth had nothing to accuse him of. She suspected that he might have had some influence over Mr Bingley's abandonment of Jane, though she had no proof of that. Regardless, Mr Bingley was with him when Mr Darcy came for her, and so the truth of the business mattered little.

And the disparaging whispers of some *others* must also be disregarded. Mr Wickham had accused Mr Darcy of many sins, but his own attempt to cajole her into relinquishing her chastity had forever lowered Elizabeth's opinion of that blackguard. Someone with morals so disconnected from propriety and virtue would have no trouble deceiving others in order to raise his own consequence and engender the sympathies of his acquaintances. As Mr Darcy had never shown any indications of immoral conduct, Elizabeth was forced to conclude that Mr Wickham's tales of woe had been at least exaggerated, possibly entirely fabricated. Perhaps she would ask Mr Darcy about it, but not so soon after he had performed such a great act of devotion.

Elizabeth owed Mr Darcy respect and more. She would make every effort to engage her affections for him since it was clear he cared about her so very much—at least for now. She did worry that this was an infatuation that would naturally ebb and he would ultimately regret, but she would devote herself to the task of being a good wife to forestall that eventuality. She would not wish to pollute his good name further than their elopement already had, nor the shades of his grand estate. If she could love him, she would. Elizabeth was determined.

Just when Elizabeth thought they were to travel the entire distance to Scotland without any conversation at all, Mr Darcy broke the silence.

"You look lovely, Miss Bennet. In your wedding gown, I mean."

His eyes were more steadily fixed upon her now, and his fingers, balled up into a fist, rested quietly against his knee. It seemed he had built up his courage to converse, and Elizabeth, despite all the emotions warring within her, was charmed by his vulnerability.

"I thank you, sir."

"Not that you are not always lovely, of course," he said, his nervousness rising once more. He cleared his throat and shifted anew. Elizabeth experienced a small thrill whenever a part of him brushed against her, and this time was no different.

"Indeed, it has been many weeks since…since I have considered you one of the handsomest women of my acquaintance."

"Oh?" Elizabeth was perplexed by the admission, though she supposed she should not be; if he was so desperate to marry her as to scoop her up and make for the border, one must naturally assume that he found her attractive. Considering his previous statements to the contrary, however, she was sceptical out of pure habit. Still, it was not the sort of thing with which a lady confronted her newly betrothed. After all, they were not so far from Longbourn that Mr Darcy could not turn the carriage round and return her to her family. So, all she said was "Thank you."

He placed a reverent kiss upon her fingers, lingering there an extra moment. "I assure you, my dearest, loveliest Elizabeth, I shall do everything in my power to make you happy in our life together. Do not take my earlier removal from Netherfield to mean that I am not devoted to your every want and need, because I am. I deeply regret the cowardice that took me from your side and left you vulnerable to others' machinations, and swear to you that nothing of the sort will ever happen again. How you must have suffered in my absence!"

Elizabeth knew not how to reply, so she simply stared at their conjoined hands. *Mr Darcy is under the misapprehension that some sort of attachment has existed between us these past weeks!*

Perhaps encouraged by her nearness, Mr Darcy leant closer and said, "I will admit that I had reservations about proposing, but my affection for you has pushed all of that aside. I could not stand by and allow you to marry another, especially one such as Mr Collins, no matter your family's want of propriety or the inferiority of your connexions." Mr Darcy smiled at her here as if expecting praise for his magnanimity, but Elizabeth clenched her teeth tightly in order to hold back a dozen insults.

"And I am certain, once the dust has settled, that we shall brave the scorn of society perfectly well, in spite of your relations."

As Mr Darcy blithely expounded upon his adoration and the various obstacles he had overcome to make his grand gesture, Elizabeth fought against every urge to lash out against him. Much as he had at the Meryton assembly, which seemed so long ago, Mr Darcy insulted her most grievously without seeming to be aware of it. How could he pronounce his love for her in one breath and denounce her as unsuitable in the next? *Arrogant, horrible man.*

She closed her eyes and concentrated on the galloping thud of her heart, a method that always calmed her when she was anxious or troubled. In this instance, she was both, and so it took some intense application to slow her pulse and regain control of the tongue that longed to give Mr Darcy a set-down he would not soon forget. Much as she wished to do so, though, this was hardly the time or the place to instigate a quarrel; despite his offensive comments, she felt she owed Mr Darcy much, and it would still be some hours yet before they could stop for the evening. It was best to contain her hurt pride for the present.

"Are you well?"

When Elizabeth opened her eyes, Mr Darcy was staring at

her with what she thought might be concern. Her previous attempts at reading him, however, had been notably poor, and so she would not assume. "Yes, only a bit of a headache. It has been an eventful morning." And so it had. Now that the words were out of her mouth, she realised that she did, in fact, suffer from a dull ache behind her eyes.

"Why not rest, then?" Mr Darcy suggested, a small smile lifting the corners of his lips. It made him look unusually handsome, Elizabeth decided against her will.

Oh, would her internal conflict never cease? One minute full of gratitude and tenderness for the man beside her, the next infuriated by him, only to return to being utterly smitten by his guileless solicitude. Mr Darcy inspired powerful, contradictory emotions within Elizabeth's breast, and they all seemed determined to fight it out. In the end, which would reign supreme? Admiration or annoyance? Love or loathing?

She knew not her own mind, and resting seemed a better alternative to acrimonious conversation or fraught silence. "I think I shall."

After pulling her hand free of his and tucking it beneath her rug, Elizabeth sank more deeply into the upholstery and closed her eyes, though she could not sleep. The silence prevailed thereafter until they stopped for the night.

CHAPTER TWELVE

They stopped just as twilight was falling across the landscape. As their journey was unplanned, the inn that Darcy's driver chose was unfamiliar, but it appeared clean and respectable, and there were enough rooms available that Elizabeth and Darcy could have one each. Thus, it would do. The proprietor was exceptionally accommodating to 'Mr and Mrs Darcy'—they must pose as already married for propriety's sake—if a touch overeager. He was perhaps a bit overawed to be hosting such wealthy clientele, and many hints were required before he ceased his obsequious attentions and left them to their meal.

Their awkwardly silent meal.

In a small sitting room which adjoined Elizabeth's bedchamber, the pair ate with the same excruciating muteness that had plagued them for much of the day. Aside from the common courtesies, necessary communications, and a short conversation in which Darcy had asked after Elizabeth's headache and she had dully murmured that it was better, neither had said much. He had not expected his vivacious Elizabeth, who appeared comfortable in every sort of company, to be so very dull. Instead of teasing him in her usual sportive manner, she pushed her dinner about with her spoon, acting in a reticent manner more akin to his own wont.

Darcy observed her more closely. She looked fatigued and, if her pinched expression was anything to judge by, a headache was still plaguing her. Anxiously, he hoped it truly was the pain and not his presence that troubled her. As the hours crept by without any signs of the sparkling wit and vivacity that had drawn him to her in the first place, he began to fear that what ailed her was not physical.

"How is your head?" he blurted again.

Elizabeth did not bother looking up from her stew as she answered in a listless whisper, "A little better, I think."

Darcy knew not what else to say. She should be happy! Had he not rescued her from her lot as Mrs Collins and all the horrors that entailed? Had he not promised her everything he had to offer, his heart as well as his consequence and wealth? What had she left behind other than misery?

Her family. Of course Elizabeth would miss them, regardless of their improprieties. And perhaps she also felt some remorse for the way she had abandoned them. They had, after all, expected her to marry the heir and preserve Longbourn for their sake, and she had instead run from the altar. Once he and Elizabeth could send word that their impromptu trip to Scotland had indeed ended in marriage, Darcy was certain the

Bennets would find it in their collective hearts to forgive her. It would all be well.

In the meantime, it was his duty to soothe his bride's concerns, however ill qualified he felt to do so. He cleared his throat, and Elizabeth immediately ceased picking at her food to look up at him. *My, but she looks so lovely, even after a day spent in a carriage and so much worry on her shoulders.*

After coughing again, Darcy said, "I wanted to reassure you that, once we are married, we can begin reconciliation with your family."

She blinked rapidly at him in surprise. "Oh? I had not thought...I thank you, sir."

"Under the circumstances, perhaps you might call me Fitzwilliam? At least when we are alone."

She nodded but made no immediate attempt to use his Christian name.

Very well. Back to the topic of her family. "We might pay them a visit in the spring, before the Season begins."

For the first time in hours, a weak smile appeared on Elizabeth's countenance. "I would very much like that, if it would be no trouble."

"No trouble at all," he assured her in a more animated tone, emboldened by her response. "I am certain Bingley will not mind putting us up at Netherfield."

"Could we not stay at Longbourn?"

Darcy fought the compulsion to fidget under her wide, hopeful regard. "Ah, perhaps, though I suspect we would be more comfortable at Netherfield."

Elizabeth's mouth thinned into a line. "I see."

"And mayhap, once your sister is married to Bingley, we might see her in town."

Much to Darcy's relief, Elizabeth brightened again. "Does he mean to offer for her, then?"

"That was his intention, yes. I should not be surprised if they are already engaged."

This pronouncement was rewarded with a soft exclamation of joy. "I knew it! I knew he loved her. Does Mr Bingley have a house in town? I should love to have Jane near me."

"Not as yet, although I suspect he will be in the market for one soon. In the meantime, an invitation to Darcy House would not be out of the question." Once they had been afforded a month or two to themselves, of course; no man wanted relations underfoot so early in his marriage. *At least I do not*, Darcy thought as his eyes caressed Elizabeth's glowing visage in the candlelight.

"It would be absolutely lovely to have the Bingleys in residence," Elizabeth said, warming to Darcy's suggestion. "We might also invite my aunt and uncle to dinner. I suppose you did not get to properly meet them earlier, but I assure you they are entirely delightful. I suspect I shall hardly get to see them at all once we have decamped to Derbyshire, although my aunt Gardiner would not be opposed to visiting Lambton. She lived there as a girl."

Darcy's gut clenched. He had heard much of Elizabeth's extended family from Miss Bingley, and none of her reports had been particularly flattering. "Your aunt and uncle from Cheapside?"

Elizabeth's radiance dimmed perceptibly, and her eyes

narrowed. "*Near* Cheapside, yes. My mother's brother and his wife. They are wonderful people, exceedingly genteel. I think you will like them."

"I am certain you are correct, however..."—Darcy sucked in a sharp breath and steeled himself to disappoint his beloved —"I believe it best at this juncture to limit our association with...that is, it would not be appropriate to..."

Elizabeth threw her napkin down next to her largely uneaten meal and glared at him. "You do not wish me to recognise my own aunt and uncle? And after they showed us such support against Mr Collins?"

Darcy sighed. "I am sorry, my love, but on this point I must be firm. You will have enough difficulty finding acceptance amongst my circle without parading about your relations in trade. In time, after the scandal of our elopement has died down, perhaps you might visit them on occasion. However, to invite them to our home as if they are our equals is out of the question."

Elizabeth opened her mouth, then abruptly snapped it closed again. The way her jaw clenched and eyes flashed beneath furrowed brows implied she was cross with him, but Darcy knew his concerns were valid. *Perhaps I could have been more tactful, though.*

Without another word, she stood and muttered, "If you would excuse me, I am for bed. Goodnight."

Leaping up from his own seat, Darcy exclaimed, "Forgive me, it pains me to offend you, but I am only thinking of your best interests."

Elizabeth stopped short and made a sceptical, unladylike sound of derision. "That I very much doubt."

"I beg your pardon?"

But Elizabeth would say no more and again attempted to extricate herself from the room. "I really must lie down. My head aches most painfully."

"Please, dearest," Darcy blocked her exit by stepping in front of her and placing both of his hands on her shoulders. "I beg you would not dissemble with me. I know I have distressed you and am sorry to have done so, but soon you will be my wife, and it is my duty to protect your reputation, especially after I myself have sullied it. We must be careful."

Elizabeth lifted her face to look at him directly, her magnificent eyes shiny with unshed tears. "Then tell me why."

"Why?" Darcy repeated, puzzled by her challenge.

"Why do you wish to marry me? If my family and I are so beneath you and your consequence, why would you risk everything to make me your wife? Would it not have been better to leave me to Mr Collins?"

This accusation struck Darcy like a physical blow. He dropped his hands from Elizabeth and staggered back a step. "What?"

The tears that had threatened to fall now overflowed and cascaded down her cheeks. "Ever since I entered your carriage this morning, you have made it abundantly clear how much you disdain every one of my relations. You were not more eloquent on the subject of tenderness than of your pride! Your sense of my inferiority—of our marriage being a degradation! With every passing hour, I see new evidence of your regret."

Though Darcy wished to disclaim Elizabeth's accusations with enough eloquence to put her at ease, his own perturbation prevented the words from forming. All he could manage was a weak rebuttal. "I assure you that is not true."

Elizabeth scoffed. "Is it not? You can barely speak to me save to serve me an insult or, contrarily, assure me of a regard I have never seen for myself. You say that you are in love with me, yet all I recall of our past association is your open disdain for me."

Too confounded to be properly offended by her speech, Darcy gave a faltering objection. "I-I have never disdained you!"

"No?" Elizabeth raised a sceptical eyebrow. "Did you not, on the evening we were first in company together, refuse to dance with me and say I was not handsome enough to tempt you? If I was meant to take such as a compliment, forgive me for misinterpreting your *good opinion*!"

Darcy felt his ears warm as mortification crashed over him. He had hoped—in vain, it appeared—that she had not overheard that little *bon mot*. "I...my opinion has changed vastly since then. Is that not obvious?"

"If you mean our elopement, yes, I suppose it is," Elizabeth conceded, albeit morosely. "However, your manner of recommending yourself to me could be improved. It, again, leads me to wonder why, with such evident a desire to marry me, you chose to tell me how unworthy I am to be your bride. Truly, Mr Darcy, it seems that I was more correct when I believed you indifferent to me."

Darcy stiffened. "And this is your opinion of me? I must

wonder, then, that you chose to abscond with me at all, if you were so certain of my disesteem before today."

"How could I think otherwise?" Elizabeth threw up her arms in exasperation. Tears dripped from the point of her chin, but she hardly seemed to notice it.

"I fell to my knees in the dirt and begged you to marry me! Then, when it appeared we might be thwarted, I swept you up and embarked upon an elopement. I did all this against my will, against my reason, and even against my character! Do you suppose I would have gone so far if I did not feel the very deepest love for you?" Darcy all but shouted at her.

The private sitting room was silent for several long, tortuous minutes save for the rapid breathing of the two combatants.

At length, Elizabeth spoke, her voice warbling and strained. "My concern, sir, is that the love you feel for me now is not so deep as you suppose, and that once this adventure has concluded and we are settled into our lives together, you will find yourself dissatisfied with the choice you have made."

So saying, Elizabeth rushed past him, a soft sob in her throat, and fled the room. This time, Darcy did nothing to stop her.

———— ⚜ ————

DARCY RETREATED TO HIS OWN ROOM AND SPENT THE NEXT hour pacing back and forth across the constrained space, feeling much like a caged lion. What could Elizabeth mean by asking him why he wished to marry her? Was the answer not obvious? Gentlemen did not simply interrupt weddings and whisk away unhappy brides as a matter of routine. Did not his actions speak for him?

And how could she ever have got the impression that he disdained her? Aside from one unfortunate comment—spoken in a moment of pique at Bingley's incessant entreaties that Darcy ought to dance—had his gaze not followed Elizabeth like a lovelorn puppy? Had he not granted her his rapt attention whenever they were in company together? Had he not shown her marked attentions at the Netherfield ball?

He felt some remorse over speaking so openly of his disgust of her family, but even there Darcy felt some measure of vindication. His feelings were natural and just. How could Elizabeth expect him to congratulate himself on joining a family whose situation in life was so decidedly beneath his own? Not only that, but their behaviour at times was absolutely atrocious. No, she could not expect him to be ashamed of his opinions, even if he had, perhaps, related them poorly.

Darcy felt he should be aggrieved, yet all he could muster was weariness after such a long day. Weariness, guilt, and an overwhelming sense of frustration. Had this elopement been an enormous mistake? Was he binding himself forever to a woman who clearly did not love him as he did her? Darcy's heart clenched as if caught within a fist at the thought. A small, dainty fist which he had foolishly placed within his own chest.

It already was far too late to do anything other than make

for Scotland. There was no going back, especially for Elizabeth; only ruination lay behind, and so they must forge on. For better or worse, Darcy must see this through until the bitter end.

Having finally exhausted his agitated spirits into despondency, Darcy abandoned his pacing and changed into his nightshirt, knowing he must at least attempt to sleep. After extinguishing his candle and climbing into bed, he closed his eyes and pondered how he was to face another long day confined in a carriage with a woman whom he apparently did not understand at all. The image of Elizabeth's fine eyes overflowing with tears remained with him in his troubled dreams.

CHAPTER THIRTEEN

The next morning, Elizabeth's bleary eyes fluttered open very much against her will as she came into wakefulness. She was unsure of her whereabouts, and her head felt stuffed with cotton. *It is early,* was her only coherent thought.

There was a knock at her door—a door that looked unfamiliar to her sleep-heavy eyes—and a low voice called out. "Miss B—Mrs Darcy, are you awake?"

The voice was deep and mellifluous. Despite its attempt to rouse her, the soothing sound made her nestle deeper into her pillow. It could not be speaking to her, as she was not Mrs Darcy.

The voice called again, accompanied by a staccato of sharp raps. "Come, our breakfast has arrived." Elizabeth groaned and rolled to her side.

After a long moment of blessed quiet—she presumed that

this unknown Mrs Darcy had answered her summons—Elizabeth settled back into repose. With a soft sigh, she drifted happily into a pleasant dream full of shy smiles and a pair of penetrating silver eyes.

"*Elizabeth.*"

She startled into full alertness at the insistent jostling of her shoulder and vaulted upright, biting back a scream. Looming over her, with one hand holding a lit candle and the other just withdrawing from her person, was Mr Darcy.

"Sir! What do you do in my bedchamber?"

Mr Darcy flushed and glanced over his shoulder into the room beyond, where an elderly woman was busy setting out their morning repast. She seemed not to have heard Elizabeth's outburst or, if she had, was apparently content to pay it no heed.

"Forgive me for invading your privacy, but you must rise. 'Tis already quarter past seven, and we should be on our way soon," Mr Darcy said. His bearing was stiff and oddly formal, and his grey eyes darted about without landing on any particular object. They avoided her entirely.

In a rush, memories from yesterday flooded into Elizabeth's mind. Mr Collins. The wedding. The elopement. Mr Darcy. *The quarrel.* She squeezed her eyes shut and rubbed her forehead as recollections throbbed between her temples. "I shall dress and join you in a moment."

"Very good."

His footsteps retreated, the door closed, and Elizabeth was alone once more. She flopped back onto the mattress.

I must apologise to Mr Darcy for my abominable behaviour last night!

There had been no call to lash out at him as she had, especially after he had done her such a good turn. Her only excuse was that the day before had been so trying and emotional that she had hardly known what to feel by the end of it. After a night of rest and the abatement of her headache, everything was much clearer: she was utterly grateful for Mr Darcy's intervention.

Perhaps her suitor could have conveyed his sentiments in a more amiable manner, but Elizabeth was willing to overlook a few shortcomings. Truly, though his denigration of her family was not at all to her liking, could she entirely blame him for feeling that way? Had she herself not lamented their vulgarity and impropriety many a time? And had her father's indolence and indecision not led to the very situation in which she found herself?

Unlike her, Mr Darcy had not the advantage of affection to mitigate her family's shortcomings. It was her task to make him see past their defects and appreciate the wonderful, loving people beneath their imperfections if she hoped to see them with any regularity in the future. And he had promised her that they might visit in the spring, had he not? That was…something. She only hoped that they might return to Longbourn before Mr Bennet departed this world.

Her eyes began to sting at the thought, and she furiously blinked away the tears that threatened to form. There was no time for that. She must dress then break her fast with Mr Darcy so they could continue their journey. December's weather was notoriously fickle, and it would only get worse the farther north they went. They needed to cover as much ground as possible in case Mother Nature decided to make mischief.

She threw off her blankets with a sweep of an arm and froze, realising for the first time that Mr Darcy had seen her in nothing but her nightrail. She loosed a nervous giggle at the thought. *No wonder he would not look at me!*

———— ◦⋙✕⋘◦ ————

A SHORT TIME LATER, ELIZABETH WAS WASHED, DRESSED, AND as ready as she ever would be to face Mr Darcy. She hesitated at the door and nibbled at her thumbnail, anxious over how she would be received. Was he regretting his choice? Might he be plotting how to discreetly send her home?

Well, fretting will change nothing. I must face him sooner or later. After steeling her courage, she opened the door. On the other side, the small table at which they had taken their disastrous dinner was laid with a new meal. The tea service was set out, toast and pots of jam enticed her empty belly, and there was a plate of pleasingly plump sausages as well. All of it looked and smelled delicious.

Mr Darcy was standing at the window and peering out, a cup of tea in one hand. He remained perfectly still and, from his reflection in the windowpane, Elizabeth could see that his

expression was similarly rigid. She swallowed with apprehension.

"Good morning, sir."

Mr Darcy reanimated at her greeting, turning to face her.
"Good morning, madam. I trust you slept well?"

Elizabeth nearly gasped at how wan he appeared in the
dawning light, how dark the circles under his eyes were. Guilt
stirred within her, growling in Mr Darcy's defence. *Just look
at what you have done to him!*

In a small voice, she replied, "I did. And you?"

"Well enough." It was an obvious prevarication. "Do sit
down and eat. We shall not be stopping for several hours."

As he began to turn back to the window, Elizabeth rushed
forward and touched his arm, halting his movement. "I must
beg your forgiveness for the things I said. I am not as
ungrateful as you must believe me to be, I promise you. Truly,
it was merely a difficult day and I unfairly unleashed my frustration upon you. First thinking I was to be tied to Mr Collins,
then the surprise of your arrival, and my father…" Her voice
rasped with feeling as she concluded, "I am more sorry than I
can say."

Mr Darcy observed her for an extended, tortuous moment
before his countenance softened appreciably and his shoulders
loosened, apparently relieved of some invisible tension. "I must
accept my share of the blame. I might have wished for a gentler
reprimand, but you were not incorrect when you accused me of
belittling you. It had not occurred to me that you might take
what I said in such a light, and I hope you might reciprocate

with your own forgiveness." He tentatively took Elizabeth's hand. "I should never have implied that marrying you would be a degradation, or that you were unworthy in any way. If that were the case, I should not be half so in love with you as I am."

Elizabeth found herself profoundly touched by Mr Darcy's sentiments, despite her lingering doubts over their longevity. "My forgiveness is yours, sir. I thank you for being so willing to put our disagreement behind us." *Perhaps his resentment is not so implacable, after all.*

Mr Darcy raised the hand he had captured to his lips and bestowed upon it a lingering kiss. Elizabeth's cheeks burned both at the sensation and the intensity with which Mr Darcy observed her. She was suddenly reminded of this morning's dream as his eyes, gleaming nearly silver in the first light of morning, regarded her searchingly.

"I fear there is still much to discuss," Elizabeth said, her voice emerging as a squeak, "but at least we have a great deal of time before us to do so."

"Indeed," agreed Mr Darcy, lowering her hand but not relinquishing it. He then led her to the table where their break-fast was laid out. "For now, let us eat and be on our way."

———— ✖ ————

WHILE DARCY AND ELIZABETH HAD EXCHANGED PLEASANT, IF somewhat stilted, conversation over their tea and toast, an hour into their journey they were returned to the previous day's tense silence. She could barely look at him, while he had fallen back to his former habit of surreptitious staring. Darcy was more frustrated with himself than her, for she had at least broached the topic of their disagreement that morning. He felt all the pressure of making the next move, yet knew not where to begin.

In his mind, he tested out a few potential topics, each more pointless than the last. He dismissed an enquiry about the weather as terribly dull, a compliment on her gown would be insipid, and another apology for his prior incivility was more likely to dig his grave deeper than appease her.

He furtively regarded her from across the carriage—he had not dared assume that he was welcome to sit beside her after learning how little she held him in affection. She nibbled on the corner of her thumbnail while gazing out the window, her eyes skimming the passing scenery without appearing to actually see it.

She was obviously anxious, and why should she not be? She must think him lost to all proper feeling to have abused her so the day before. Oh, he could rationalise that his sentiments were natural and just, that he had merely meant to illustrate how deeply he adored her, but he had hurt her. Far more than her anger, it was her tears that undid him. *Good God, I made her cry.*

Darcy shook himself to dispel the sudden surge of shame that rushed in; self-flagellation was not productive, and he had much better focus on proving to Elizabeth that she was not making an enormous mistake. He cleared his throat, but having gained Elizabeth's attention without really knowing what to do with it, he blurted the first thought that entered his head. "Are you comfortable?"

Excellent, man. A far better topic than the weather.

Elizabeth offered him a soft smile; perhaps she sympathised with his awkwardness. "Yes, I am most comfortable. This is an excellent vehicle for a long journey."

"Indeed it is. I find it necessary for my frequent trips from Pemberley to London and back again."

"Mm."

Darcy's mind worked frantically to fill the growing void between them. "Elizabeth, I…that is, it seems to me that we should spend our journey getting better acquainted. We are to be married, after all, and it would be best to know a little something of each other beforehand."

The slow, wry curl of Elizabeth's lips surprised him; he did not think he had said anything amusing. Had it been anyone other than Elizabeth, he might have been affronted.

"Forgive me, sir, I am not laughing at you. It is only that my friend Charlotte has often espoused exactly the *opposite* view of courtship. Truthfully, I am much more inclined to your view of things than hers, and anticipate a greater familiarity with you."

Elizabeth's soft tease released much of Darcy's tension. This was more what he had expected from her; this he could respond to.

Eagerness welling up within him, he straightened in his seat and leant towards her. "I asked you last night not to dissemble with me, and I meant it. If you are ever vexed with me or have a concern, I beg that you would speak your mind. I would have us be entirely open with one another."

She regarded him steadily, her expression more sober than he had ever observed. "Even if what I have to say, you would not wish to hear?"

"Especially then."

She inhaled a deep breath and released it slowly. "I shall hold you to that, sir, but I think it best to begin with an easy question: How did you come to know of my betrothal to Mr Collins?"

"Miss Bingley. Your sister wrote to her of your upcoming nuptials." Darcy proceeded to tell Elizabeth the story of Miss Bingley's recitation and was rewarded with a merry giggle. He swelled with pride at the amusement sparkling in Elizabeth's eyes. It was a heady feeling to have inspired it.

"Miss Bingley will not like to hear of your marriage to *Miss Eliza*, and less that she herself has brought it about. Oh, that is too rich! She will never forgive herself."

Darcy could not help but join Elizabeth in her diversion. Miss Bingley had pursued him mercilessly since her come out, and only his friendship with Bingley had prevented him from saying something horribly rude to dissuade her.

"And I assume she will be less than pleased to hear of her brother's betrothal to Jane?"

"I would imagine so."

"Poor Miss Bingley."

"Save your sympathy, for she has none for you. She gloated and cackled over your engagement to Mr Collins, knowing how miserable your life would be. Even had I not been in love with you, I would have been far too disgusted to ever offer for the likes of *her*."

Elizabeth's cheeks flushed, and she averted her gaze. Darcy panicked, wondering what he had said to cause her to withdraw again. But before he could blindly apologise, she asked in a soft voice, "How did you come to fall in love with me?"

Darcy had never before considered the origin of his attachment; he had only fought fruitlessly to suppress it before fate intervened. He replied with the awkward, unvarnished truth. "I...I cannot fix on the hour, or the spot, or the look, or the words, which laid the foundation. I was in the middle before I knew that I had begun."

One corner of Elizabeth's mouth tilted up even as she kept her gaze on her lap. "My beauty you had early withstood, and as for my manners—my behaviour to you was at least always bordering on the uncivil, and I never spoke to you without rather wishing to give you pain than not. I cannot fathom how you might have come to so much as like me, much less build an affection that could provoke you into disrupting my wedding. How could you begin? What could have set you off in the first place?"

Sensing that his reply would be important, the sort that could either inspire tenderness or hinder its formation, Darcy took some time to gather his thoughts. At length he said, "I would give you an explanation if I could, but one escapes me. Your wit, your vivacity, and, yes, your beauty have ensnared me, no matter what nonsensical thing I said out of misplaced spite. I have truly never known another woman like you, Elizabeth. Not one lady in the entire *ton*."

"There are no other ladies of your acquaintance with such staggering disregard for your dignity, sir? None with so much impertinence?"

Elizabeth's jest was a weak one, filled with uncertainty, but Darcy was charmed by it all the same. "None with your liveliness of mind. They are all insipid and dull next to you."

"Oh, I see. You are disgusted with the women who are always speaking and looking and thinking for your approbation alone. I have roused and interested you because I am so unlike them. I suspect you are far more amiable than I have given you credit for because, were you not, you would hate me for it. There —I have saved you the trouble of accounting for it and, really, all things considered, I begin to think it perfectly reasonable."

Darcy laughed at this portrait of himself. "I might not have put it in such a way myself, but I shall not deny there is some truth to your assertions. I cannot like hearing my own opinions reflected back at me. I much prefer a challenge."

Straightening his features, Darcy continued, more seriously this time, "You mentioned some concern that in the future I might grow dissatisfied with you as my wife, and I want to assure you that it will not be so. My love for you may not be of long duration, but neither is it the work of a moment. I have come to care for you as I have no one else. I have no regrets over coming back for you, only that I did not do so sooner so that we might have averted this necessity to elope. Had I been less of a coward and remained in Hertfordshire to court you openly, you might never have been subjected to a forced betrothal."

"You cannot know that. Had I not been required to entertain an engagement to Mr Collins, you might never have come to the point. If you had, I might not have welcomed your advances. I believe all has turned out as it should."

Darcy's heart warmed at her sanguinity, although he ultimately remained dissatisfied. "I...I know that you cannot return my feelings at the present, but I hope, one day, that you might...that is, do you think you could...?"

Elizabeth placed her hand atop his. "I have every intention of growing to love you, Fitzwilliam. Even if your admiration for me fades over time, I shall become the best wife I can possibly be."

As if Darcy could ever stop loving her when she regarded him with such promise in her eyes and his Christian name on her lips. "In the meantime, I shall devote myself to earning your love, my dearest, loveliest Elizabeth."

CHAPTER FOURTEEN

The couple spent the next several hours in pleasant, lively discussions about everything and nothing. Elizabeth was surprised to discover that she and Mr Darcy were of the same mind on many topics and, when they were not, their debates were thoughtful and good-natured. Unlike many men, he truly listened to her opinions and was willing to consider what she said without undue prejudice. To her amusement and his mortification, it transpired that he had already catalogued many of her likes and dislikes over the course of their relatively short acquaintance. He had successfully guessed her favourite colour was yellow, noted her preference for pheasant over fish, and commended her habits of frequent exercise. He was also aware of her disinclination for lace, though she had no earthly idea how he had discerned it. Did gentlemen often pay such close heed to a lady's wardrobe? Apparently, his penchant for staring at her had paid off, which was at turns sweet and a tad unsettling.

It also put Elizabeth at somewhat of a disadvantage because she had few such observations of the gentleman. Certainly, she knew how he took his coffee and had noted a penchant for green in his attire, but her pretence of sketching his character had not revealed more than that. She had been content to give him her attention only when he demanded it of her and no more.

At least they were on even footing when it came to subjects of greater import, such as their opinions on literature, the ongoing war, and the importance of family, however maddening the latter proved to be. When Elizabeth asked him to tell her about his, Mr Darcy tilted his head as he pondered his response. She bit her lip lest she giggle at how adorably lopsided he looked.

"There is sadly not much to tell. My sister, Georgiana, is the only member of my immediate family who remains to me."

Elizabeth's heart lurched at the matter-of-fact way he announced this. "Are you not close to any of your aunts and uncles? Cousins?"

"There are so few Darcys left, and we are so scattered about the country that we are hardly known to one another. The only one with whom I ever had much contact was my great-uncle James, who was a judge and remained a bachelor until his death some years ago."

"What about your mother's family?"

Mr Darcy grimaced but quickly smoothed his features

again. "My mother's family is a mixed blessing. While I am fond of my cousin Richard—a colonel in the army, you would like him, I think—with others I cannot seem to achieve the same sort of closeness. My other cousin, the Viscount Marbury, is interested only in his own pursuits, not all of which I can approve. As for their sister, Lady Smithfield, I have been forced to maintain a careful distance since her come out. Even before that, she was far too young to make a boon companion."

"I believe your uncle is an earl?" Elizabeth vaguely recalled hearing from Miss Bingley that his grandfather had been one, but it had not occurred to her how closely related Mr Darcy was to the peerage. To her, he had always been an ordinary, albeit wealthy, gentleman. No doubt his elevated kin would be displeased to hear of his elopement with a simple country girl with no fortune and connexions to trade. She experienced a surge of self-doubt before tamping it down; regardless of the rank of Mr Darcy's relations, he was a gentleman, she a gentleman's daughter. In that regard they were equal.

"Yes, he is. Lord Matlock is a decent enough man, but he is nearly always in London to advance his political aspirations. We see each other occasionally during the Season, but I much prefer to be in the country the rest of the year."

Elizabeth fixed him with a saucy look, full of teasing vindication. "Oh, so you prefer country to town after all? I recall a *certain* gentleman abusing the confined and unvarying society of a country neighbourhood."

He awarded her the point with surprising good humour.

"You have caught me out. However, I defy anyone to prefer the foggy, stinking streets of London over the rugged beauty of the Peaks. You will be of my opinion once you have seen Pemberley for yourself."

"I do not dispute it, sir. It is well known that I am a country girl at heart. But what of Lady Matlock? Are you fond of her?"

"She is pleasant enough, although I was forced to avoid her for several years after I came into my inheritance because she cherished a desire for me to marry her daughter. Though I suppose I am safe now that Frederica is married to Lord Smithfield."

"My goodness, you are absolutely beset by matchmaking aunts!" She laughed at the absurdity.

Mr Darcy joined in her merriment with a wry chuckle. "You might say that. Although Lady Catherine does indeed expect me to lead Anne to the altar eventually, I have always resisted it. I swear that I have never been engaged to her, nor was I ever tempted to propose, so do not believe a word your cousin says. I have not broken a contract or jilted anyone to be here."

Elizabeth gave him a rueful grin. "No, I suppose that singular honour falls to me."

She realised that her jest had landed amiss when Mr Darcy's countenance paled noticeably. "Oh, Elizabeth, I did not mean—"

In contrition, she reached across the carriage and placed her hand upon his forearm. "Forgive me. I did not mean it as censure of our behaviour. Perhaps I *should* feel that we have done wrong, but I have little compassion for Mr Collins, who insisted upon my marrying him even after I rejected his initial proposal. I suspect he did so out of spite, and thus cannot muster any remorse for leaving him at the altar."

Mr Darcy's features tightened into a configuration of outrage. "You rejected his proposal, and he still forced you into a betrothal?"

"He did indeed, which absolves me of much of the guilt I should be experiencing presently. But as I said before, I believe all has turned out as it should."

Mr Darcy openly seethed, and it seemed safest to resume the topic of his family. "Tell me about your parents. Were you close to them?"

"To my mother, sadly, no." He accompanied this revelation with a long sigh. "She was as affectionate as she knew how to be, but the Fitzwilliams have never been an especially warm brood. We might have got to know one another better as I grew into manhood, but unfortunately she died giving birth to my sister sixteen years ago."

"I am so sorry." What must it be like to lose your mother at such a young age? By Elizabeth's calculation, Mr Darcy must have been twelve or thirteen when his mother died, barely old enough to truly know her. Much as Mrs Bennet often chafed Elizabeth's nerves, and as frequently as she mortified her daughters with her vulgar behaviour, she had at least assisted them all through the most turbulent years of their collective adolescence. From her mother, Elizabeth had learnt to hold her head high and let no one's opinion tarnish her own self-worth, a trait that had been invaluable when a certain gentleman disparaged her appearance at a dance in the not so distant past.

Mr Darcy's expression softened. "I thank you, but it was so long ago that I hardly dwell on it now. I often wish she were still alive for Georgiana's sake, but I have made peace with her absence."

Elizabeth could not believe that he did not miss his mother, but she allowed him the comfort that the prevarication offered. "And your father?"

Pain flashed across his face, and Elizabeth instantly regretted her query.

"I was fortunate enough to be close to my father, even if we had our…disagreements later on. He died five years ago, and his absence is keenly felt."

A burning sensation presaged the tears that quickly filled Elizabeth's eyes. For the second time that day, she attempted to quell them, but they came too rapidly to be stopped. In an effort to hide her grief, she turned her head to stare out of the window.

"Elizabeth?"

The concern in Mr Darcy's voice was tinged in alarm, but as much as Elizabeth wanted to reassure him, she could not speak round the lump in her throat. A linen square appeared in her line of vision, and she accepted it with alacrity, desperate to stem the flow of tears. Would the anguish of her own father's passing be as fresh as Mr Darcy's in five years? Ten?

"Are you well? Should we stop the carriage? Truly, you look very ill."

Elizabeth abandoned the pointless endeavour of drying her

face and dropped Mr Darcy's handkerchief onto her lap. "No, that will not be necessary. It is only that when you spoke of your father, it reminded me..." Her words ended with a hiccup and a fresh wave of sorrow.

He shifted to the space beside her, and Elizabeth found that she could not object to this closeness or to his pleasant masculine scent. Nor could she object when he pulled her into his arms. If anything, he enveloped her in a circle of safety and comfort that she had not realised she needed until now. She turned into his embrace and wept into his cravat.

Once her tears at last abated, she moved to rest a cheek against his shoulder. "Forgive me. I am not usually such a watering pot. It is only that..."—she sucked in a shuddering breath—"my father is dying."

Mr Darcy's arms tightened round her. "Dying? Oh, Elizabeth."

She felt a soft pressure against the crown of her head and presumed he had placed a kiss there. "He recently found out from the apothecary. It is his heart, apparently. It is weak and could fail him at any time. It is why he insisted upon my marriage to Mr Collins."

"I admit, I had wondered about that. Your father always seemed so fond of you, and he seemed so relieved by my offer. I could not fathom why he might press you to marry a man so..."

Elizabeth emitted a shuddering sigh. "I am certain he would not have, had the situation not been so dire. Indeed, he supported my initial refusal, only to reverse it the next day when...well, it is not important."

"No, tell me."

"Well…" Elizabeth hesitated, not wishing to pain the gentleman who had so tenderly cared for her in her moment of sorrow. She suspected him of playing a role in Mr Bingley's defection from Jane, as his objections to her family were painfully clear, and hated the thought of discomfiting him. However, she had promised only that morning to be as open with him as possible, and so she must speak up. "It was after we received a note from Miss Bingley informing us that your entire party had left Netherfield forever. Apparently, Papa had been anticipating that Mr Bingley would soon offer for Jane."

Which would have saved me from accepting Mr Collins was left unsaid, but the surmise hung heavy in the air.

"So, it was all my fault." Mr Darcy clasped her yet more tightly against his chest. "I encouraged Bingley to remain in London, believing your sister indifferent to him. Had I minded my own affairs, you would not…"

"No! No, of course not!" Mr Darcy *had* behaved irresponsibly with his meddling, but nothing could have stirred Elizabeth quite so abruptly as his plaintive admission of liability. She drew back slightly so he could see the sincerity in her eyes. "Had my father not been so severely ill—something you could not have known at the time, for he hid it from everyone —I am sure we would have gone on as we were before. It was unfortunate happenstance that made me accept Mr Collins, not your actions."

"Let me feel how much I have been to blame." He looked utterly wretched, haunted even. "I am not afraid of being overcome by guilt. It is only right that I should be."

Elizabeth pressed her palm to his cheek and implored, "No, you will not take all the responsibility upon your shoulders. Others are just as culpable. I assume, from Miss Bingley's note of farewell, that his sisters also had some influence over his choices. Regardless of who persuaded him, Mr Bingley could have disregarded your advice and returned to Netherfield to discover the truth for himself. I hope, by his presence at my aborted wedding, he has decided to follow his own inclinations and do just that."

"I still cannot absolve myself for my meddling. It was not my place."

"You had no business interfering, it is true, but I suspect you were attempting to preserve your friend from an unhappy marriage—and I can understand why. I have seen the results of such a union every day of my life."

"Your parents?"

"Yes. They have been discontented with each other for as long as I can remember. It is why I have always vowed to marry for love."

Mr Darcy's eyes dimmed as abruptly as storm clouds blotting out the sun. Then he looked away. "And I have taken that from you as well."

Feeling bold, Elizabeth brought Mr Darcy's hand to her lips and pressed a soft kiss to the back of it. She noted his sharp intake of breath as she replied, "That has yet to be seen."

CHAPTER FIFTEEN

"This is really quite good," Elizabeth said, dipping her spoon into the soup and taking another sip.

"Indeed. The food here is always hearty and delicious."

After a long, frigid day of travel, a hot meal was most welcome. It had started to rain in the late afternoon, precipitously dropping the temperature outside, and Darcy's toes tingled unpleasantly as they warmed. Still, he would not complain about the cold overmuch. The adverse weather had provided him an excellent excuse to remain next to Elizabeth in the carriage. Not that she had objected to his proximity; on the contrary, she had allowed him the unprecedented honour of wrapping an arm about her shoulders as dusk fell. "For warmth," she had said with a shy smile on her tempting lips.

"You will find the accommodation here comfortable, I hope."

Elizabeth glanced over her shoulder at the privacy screen, which only partially hid the four-poster bed from view, and flushed pink.

Darcy, suddenly conscious of what she must be thinking, felt his own cheeks warm. "I shall, of course, be spending the night on the sofa." It had not been possible to secure separate rooms, but this one was large enough to boast a small seating area and a plump, inviting sofa. "You will have the bed."

"Oh, I could not…"

"I insist."

There was a long moment of hesitation from Elizabeth before she huffed a defeated laugh. "Very well."

"Thank you. I, um, enjoyed getting to know you today. Perhaps not all our topics were…happy ones, but it is a relief to be on more informal terms."

"I could not agree more, Mr—Fitzwilliam."

Elizabeth's expression held none of her former self-consciousness, and Darcy wondered if the thrill of this new familiarity would always be thus, or if he was simply a besotted buffoon and the ebullience would gradually ebb over time. He prayed it would be the former.

The quiet that descended between them thereafter was a comfortable sort, one of boon companions content simply to be in one another's presence. They continued to sup, all the while exchanging glances and bashful smiles. It was bliss.

Despite having commended the food to Elizabeth, Darcy could not eat much of it. He was far too distracted by how luminous Elizabeth looked in the candlelight, the curve of her cheek glowing a subtle gold as though gilded. A single twisting curl tickled the same cheek, bobbing impishly back in place after each of her attempts to sweep it aside. Most distracting of all, however, was the way her lips puckered to cool each spoonful, then spread slightly to sip at its contents. He was mesmerised, and could not help but envision himself leaning across the table and having a taste—though he had no interest in the soup.

"You mentioned earlier that you were close to your father."

Darcy started and shook himself; the vivid image of sampling Elizabeth's lips was slow to fade. "Forgive me, I was wool-gathering. What did you say?"

Elizabeth's eyes glittered with humour. "If you are weary of my company, I can always retire early."

"No, not at all! Pray, do speak."

"I was merely asking about your father again. You said you were close to him?"

A weight like a leaden cloak bore down upon Darcy's shoulders. He did not often speak of his father, finding it difficult to discuss a man whose passing was such a profound loss, but he would do so for Elizabeth. Not only had he promised to be entirely open with her, but she would be experiencing much the same sort of grief soon, if Mr Bennet's prognosis was truly so dire.

"I was. My father was as much a mentor to me as a parent. He taught me everything I know about estate management and instilled in me a great sense of pride in what I do. Not only because I am fortunate enough to be a Darcy and call

Pemberley my home, but because we are well-placed to do good in this world."

Elizabeth's eyes, always so expressive, softened like warm wax. "He sounds like an exceedingly good man."

"He was."

"You also mentioned that you had suffered some disagreements with him late in his life. I was wondering if…if they had aught to do with Mr Wickham?"

Darcy stiffened, temporarily frozen by the mention of his worst enemy. Some of this iciness seeped into his tone. "I suppose *he* has told you all about it."

The sweet sensation of Elizabeth's touch tingled along the back of his hand. Her eyes, which were trained upon his own, verily glowed.

"I will admit that Mr Wickham has told me some extremely disagreeable things about you," she said, "but I should like to hear your testimony. Not that I believe him any longer, since he has proved himself to be unscrupulous."

"What do you mean?" When they last spoke of Wickham at Bingley's ball, Elizabeth had openly defended the cur. Her suddenly reddened countenance was not at all reassuring.

"He…he…oh, it is too mortifying to speak of! He…he made a lewd suggestion after I became betrothed to Mr Collins. I thought he was proposing marriage at first—a prospect I had intended to reject, mind you—but that was not at all what he wanted. He suggested an…an assignation."

Had Darcy possessed less self-control, he would have sworn an oath so vile as to blister the wallpaper. Instead, he swallowed it back down, where it bubbled angrily in his stomach. "Did he touch you?"

"No! Not at all."

Perhaps Darcy could let the worm live, but only should the two men never cross paths again. If they did, Wickham would have to depend upon a higher authority to keep him in one piece. The reprobate had better hope that the Almighty was as charmed by him as young ladies seemed to be.

The sharp sound of a chair being pushed back drew Darcy out of his violent musings, and he looked up to find Elizabeth at his side. She knelt down, rested her head against his knee, and implored him with the wide set of her fine eyes. "Truly, he is not worth your concern. I only mentioned him because I felt I must know your history before we wed."

The ice and fire within Darcy's breast, which had been coalescing into a maelstrom of vengeance, were instantly subdued, and that tickling thrill he associated with Elizabeth's nearness rushed in to fill their place. He swallowed deeply, but his voice was still rough when he responded. "Very well, but let us adjourn somewhere more comfortable. 'Tis a long, complicated story."

He led her to the sofa and moved to reinvigorate the fire with the poker, but eventually he could stall no longer and settled himself next to her to begin. "Mr Wickham is the son of a very respectable man…"

Darcy told Elizabeth of all his financial dealings with Wickham without much pain or difficulty, but when he came to the blackguard's near seduction of Georgiana, his voice faltered. Elizabeth deserved to know, and he was confident he could trust her discretion, but his failures were agonising to speak of aloud. He did so, however, and was rewarded by his beloved's unreserved sympathy.

"What sort of man preys upon the innocence of a young girl to make a bit of money? He truly is an abominable, loathsome, reprehensible, revolting…libertine!"

Elizabeth's vehemence was both reassuring and endearing.

"Well, Georgiana's dowry *is* thirty thousand pounds."

She cuddled close to his side and laid her head on his shoulder. "It is no excuse. Mr Wickham is all charm without substance. Anyone with true discernment will recognise that you are the better man."

"I hardly think that is true. Even you were convinced that *I* was the villain at first."

Darcy instantly regretted his remark when he felt Elizabeth stiffen in his arms and draw away. He moved to embrace her again, but she stayed him with a hand on his chest.

"You need not tell me how foolish I was to believe Mr Wickham's fabrications on such a short acquaintance," she said, her brow furrowed in distress. "I have courted prepossession and ignorance, driven reason away, where the two of you are concerned. But this experience has taught me not to allow my vanity to rule me."

Darcy brushed that recalcitrant curl behind Elizabeth's ear. It sprang free again almost instantly, making him smile in spite of his heavier feelings. "Do not be so hard on yourself. You are hardly the only sensible person the cad has tricked. He had similar success with my father."

"Was Mr Wickham the source of your disagreement with him?"

"He was." Darcy encouraged her to come closer, and she capitulated willingly. The scent of her hair was both comforting and exhilarating. "My father did not heed my warnings that Wickham was becoming more and more profligate whilst we were away at school."

"Did he not trust your judgment?"

"I am certain he did, but we all see what we wish to see. I, myself, am not immune to this fault, though I only realised it recently." He thought of his conceited belief that Elizabeth was enamoured of him during his sojourn at Netherfield. Now that Darcy had experienced some measure of Elizabeth's true approbation and esteem, he wondered how he had overlooked the absence before.

"I see what you mean. Since my betrothal to Mr Collins, I have come to see that my father is a poor provider and does not exert himself to do things that are necessary yet difficult. I should never have been required to entertain the notion of a life as Mrs Collins, and yet here I am, fleeing from just that prospect. I know that Papa did not mean for this to happen, but the truth is that he should have stirred himself to do better by us all long before it came to this point."

Darcy rubbed soothing circles on Elizabeth's back. "I admit to thinking much the same myself. Longbourn may not be very large, but it seems prosperous enough."

Elizabeth shook her head against his chest. "I suppose it is easier to say than do, but he should have enforced stricter economy. With five daughters and no son as protection against the entail, more ought to have been set aside for our dowries. Unfortunately, my father is not well practised at denying my mother's insistent wants."

"It is humbling to grow older and realise that our parents are not as perfect as we once thought. There was a time I genuinely believed my father could do no wrong."

"I thought the same until a mere three weeks ago."

Darcy held Elizabeth even closer as their conversation gave way to quiet self-reflection. They stared into the slowly dying fire, united in their shared disappointment.

"You should go to bed," he finally said when Elizabeth yawned for the third time in as many minutes. "If you fall asleep here, you will regret it in the morning."

Elizabeth sat up enough to fix him with a saucy smile. It was particularly adorable with the way her eyes drooped in half sleep. "And you will not?"

"I shall be able to stretch out once you are abed."

"So, your motive becomes more clear! You wish me away so that you can have the sofa all to yourself."

Had this not been said with impish good humour, Darcy might have stumbled over himself to beg her pardon and correct her misapprehension. As it was, he chuckled and sallied with a quip of his own. "You have caught me out, madam. Do have the decency to vacate this area lest I think you mean to compromise my honour."

"Well!" Elizabeth said, doing a remarkable imitation of Miss Bingley with her nose pointed in the air. "I can see that I am not wanted here. Good evening, sir!"

So saying, she levered herself into a sitting position, only

7

to lose her balance and tumble directly upon Darcy's lap. He moved to assist, but in doing so they became more hopelessly entangled than ever with his foot upon the hem of her gown and Elizabeth further off-kilter. They both laughed and apologised to one another as they fought to separate. Elizabeth finally managed to extricate herself but fell on her back upon the sofa cushions. Darcy landed atop her just as clumsily, and only barely avoided crushing his beloved by catching himself with his hands on either side of her head.

Their murmurs of apology died away the moment their gazes locked. Darcy could feel all the impropriety of their current position—the sort only appropriate for a couple's wedding night—and yet he did not move a single muscle. Instead, with thrumming pulse and quickening breath, his face hovered mere inches above hers as he took in the delicious sensation of her body flush against his. He could do naught but stare at the magnificent creature beneath him.

Elizabeth's eyes were half closed, whether from fatigue or desire he knew not, and her breathing was shallow and rapid. Her lips parted slightly; he wondered whether they were about to scold him or beg him.

"Fitzwilliam—"

Without conscious thought, Darcy dipped his head to close the final distance between them and kissed her. It should have been sweet and tentative, but he was so overwhelmed by his own desire that it was more feverish than anything. Elizabeth somehow tasted more delectable than he had expected and he lapped at the seam of her lips greedily.

She gave a soft moan, one that Darcy felt down to his core.

Her fingers, which had been about his shoulders since their awkward tumble, found their way into his hair and pulled him closer against her mouth. An exquisite shiver raced down his spine, and he lowered himself more completely upon her.

Darcy only came back to his senses when a sharp pop from the fireplace startled him. He wrenched his lips away from Elizabeth's, mortified, and abruptly sat up at the edge of the sofa. What must she think of his lustful ardour? He, like Wickham, had trampled her trust. Except Wickham had never imposed himself upon her as Darcy had. His new understanding with Elizabeth, so delicately wrought throughout the day and still fragile, would crumble to nothing.

"Fitzwilliam."

Darcy glanced at her, his heart in his throat.

Elizabeth was now upright as well. She bit her lower lip, reddened and swollen from their recent activities, and her eyes were downcast. "Forgive me. I did not mean to…that is, I know I have done wrong, but—"

"Wrong! Elizabeth, it is I who should beg your forgiveness. I lost control and pounced upon you like…like…I do not wish to think how horribly I have importuned you."

Elizabeth's body seemed to sag with relief. "Oh, thank goodness! I thought I must have repulsed you with my wanton behaviour."

"No, never!"

She leant forward, hesitated, but ultimately pressed a soft kiss to his cheek. "Then it appears there is nothing for either of us to forgive. However, I do think it time for me to retire."

Much as Darcy wished otherwise, he was forced to agree.

They were not yet married, and he had far too much respect for her to anticipate their wedding vows. Or so he hoped.

CHAPTER SIXTEEN

"Might I suggest the blue, sir?"

Bingley examined the cornflower-hued waistcoat his valet held up for inspection and, struck by the similarity to his Jane's lovely eyes, nodded. "Yes, that one."

The past two days, whilst not entirely free of travail, were perhaps the happiest of Bingley's life, and it was all due to the gentle care and affection of one Jane Bennet. She was more than a pretty face; she was also kind, sweet, intelligent, and devoted to the felicity of those dear to her heart. Just look at how she had gone against society's dictates to advocate for her sister's welfare! Should he live a hundred lifetimes, he never would have believed that proper, upright Darcy would ever consider eloping, and yet Jane had convinced both him and Elizabeth to do just that. All these estimable attributes Bingley could now claim for himself, and he had every expectation of a life full of joy and contentment.

He looked at the clock to judge whether it was still too early to visit Longbourn. Perhaps a little, but the Bennets would not mind. All he longed for was to see Jane, besotted fool that he was, and the others might happily go about their own business. Yes, he would set off directly after he broke his fast.

A knock sounded at the door as Bingley slipped his arms into his waistcoat. His valet answered it; on the other side stood the butler, appearing somehow more grim and stodgy than usual. Bingley did not know how the man managed it when he already resembled a stone gargoyle.

"Mrs Hurst and Miss Bingley have just arrived, sir. They insist on an immediate audience with you."

Ah. Louisa and Caroline could darken any man's mood. With a weary sigh and a slump in his posture, Bingley replied, "Tell them I shall be down directly."

The butler bowed and departed, leaving his master full of irritation and a sense of inevitable calamity.

BINGLEY DESCENDED THE STAIRCASE A SHORT TIME LATER, practically dragging his feet along the carpet. From the upper landing, he could already hear Caroline's voice raised in shrill vexation. The interview with his sisters was not destined to be a pleasant one, but he had expected it ever since absconding from London with Darcy, leaving only a hastily dashed note behind him. They would not be best pleased to hear either that his friend was eloping with Miss Elizabeth or that he himself was engaged to Jane. Verily, their objections were sure to be vitriolic and cruel. Alas, all he could do was steel himself for the unavoidable cataclysm.

After taking a moment to straighten his cravat and fix a resolute expression upon his features, Bingley let himself into the drawing room. "Good morning, and welcome back to Netherfield Park. By your presence here, I assume you found my note. I only wonder at it taking you so long to arrive."

Both sisters immediately turned in his direction, matching scowls upon their faces. Caroline advanced upon him, but Louisa held up a hand to stay her, and she complied.

"Yes, we did," Louisa said with a sniff, "and I must say that we are most put out with you for sneaking back to Hertfordshire like some criminal. I daresay your family deserves more consideration than *that*. We would have come sooner, but your carriage apparently followed you here and Mr Hurst was away on…business"—likely meaning Hurst had gone off on one of his extended tours of debauchery—"so we were left entirely without transport until this morning. Regardless, we are here now and intent upon saving you from making a wretched mistake."

Bingley crossed his arms, feeling justifiably defiant. "Does a gentleman not have the right to return to a house he has legally hired whenever he chooses?"

Caroline, who had been pacing round the tea table, halted

mid-step and whirled to face him, white and rigid with fury. Bingley almost took a step back, but instead planted his feet and awaited her volley.

It was not long in coming. Caroline marched up to him, a finger pointing menacingly, and snarled, "Do not play coy, Charles, for we know what you are about. We have come to put a stop to this nonsense with the Bennets!"

"Nonsense?" he scoffed. "I am afraid I do not understand you. My relationship with my future family is not 'nonsense'."

"Then you have done it? You have proposed to Jane Bennet?"

Bingley puffed out his chest. "Indeed I have, and I am happy to report that she has accepted me."

"You cannot—"

"I think what Caroline means to say," Louisa interrupted with a silencing glare for her sister, "is that we are *concerned* for you. Did we not discuss this matter at length in town? Jane Bennet is hardly a suitable match when one takes into account her unfortunate connexions and small portion. And if she does not care for you, you will have thrown yourself away for nothing."

Setting his jaw, Bingley countered, "You were mistaken about Jane's feelings for me. We are in love, and I intend to make her my wife as soon as possible. We are only waiting for Darcy and Miss Elizabeth to return before Jane makes me the happiest of men."

Caroline, appearing exceedingly unwell all of a sudden, clutched at his arm. "What do you mean by 'waiting for Darcy and Miss Eliza to return'? Where is Mr Darcy?"

"He and Miss Elizabeth have eloped."

"No! It is impossible—Mr Darcy would never...could not...you *lie*!" she screeched.

Bingley winced and leant away, her objection piercing his hearing at such close range. "I am sorry for your disappointment, but it is the truth. Darcy came here with the express purpose of marrying Miss Elizabeth in her cousin's stead, and when it seemed there was a chance of Mr Collins prevailing, they felt they had no choice."

Caroline's fingernails dug so deeply into his arm that Bingley would not be surprised if she managed to somehow draw blood through his coat. There would be bruises later, for certain.

"No! No, I will not accept this! Mr Darcy cannot marry some penniless nobody—it is not fair!"

While Bingley attempted to pry Caroline's claws from his arm, Louisa darted forth to manage her sister. "Calm yourself! You are becoming overwrought."

But Caroline was descending into the sort of tantrum Bingley had not seen from her since before she was sent away to school. As a child, she had been prone to violent theatrics whenever no one catered to her whims, and she became absolutely insensible to reason during these episodes. Her education had taught her the value of ladylike deportment in achieving her ends, but apparently some of her former tendencies lingered. She was absolutely beside herself.

"Caroline, pray compose yourself," Bingley said, but his pleas went entirely unheeded; it was as if she could not hear him at all.

"Their marriage cannot possibly be legal! I am certain it will be annulled in an instant!"

"Caroline—"

"Eliza Bennet as Mrs Darcy? That country-born hoyden in *my* place as mistress of Pemberley? Never! I will never accept it!" Her speech then descended into incoherent shrieks and disjointed mutterings. It was truly alarming.

Instead of attempting to reason with his overwrought sister, which he knew would be ineffectual, Bingley turned to his other. A stronger solution must be employed. "Louisa, tell the footman to call Mr Jones."

Louisa hurried away to do as he bade, while Bingley guided Caroline to the sofa and attempted to make her sit. She resisted his exhortations, sputtering and gesticulating like a madwoman, and he prayed the apothecary would arrive soon with a calming elixir.

Glancing at the time, Bingley sighed. His visit to Longbourn would be delayed.

JANE WOULD NOT HAVE BELIEVED IT POSSIBLE, BUT Elizabeth's elopement had alleviated almost every worry in the household. There was nothing to be done about the availability of fish at the market, but otherwise the Bennets seemed content with how things had worked out. Her father, for example, appeared haler and heartier, leading Jane to conclude that the strain of their straitened circumstances had contributed to his poor health. She did not wish to raise her expectations too high, but it was impossible not to hope that Mr Jones had made a mistake and their patriarch would continue to live a great many years yet.

Mrs Bennet squawked and screeched as often as she ever did, but the topics of her nervous exclamations had shifted significantly for the better. It heartened Jane to know her mother was no longer so beset with worry. The prospect of being turned out of her home had weighed heavily on Mrs Bennet for many years; though that eventuality might still come to pass, at least now they had somewhere to go when it occurred. Between Mr Darcy and her own dear Bingley, the Bennets would be well provided for.

Kitty and Lydia were both delighted and diverted by Elizabeth's grand romantic adventure, and rejoiced that Mr Collins would not be their brother after all, even if dour Mr Darcy would take his place. However much they had disliked him before, they were apparently willing to think better of the master of Pemberley upon taking his fairy-tale rescue into due consideration.

"At least she will be rich," Lydia had remarked while Kitty bobbed her head in agreement.

Jane could not approve of their shallow values and scolded them for their unkindness, but she knew they meant well and agreed with their general sentiments—except that Mr Darcy was evidently not always dour!

Mary was the only Bennet not entirely pleased with how events had unfolded. To her mind, Elizabeth should have honoured her previous agreement by marrying Mr Collins without complaint. Mary thought it was no virtue that Elizabeth had sought her own happiness, even considering the very real misery her sister faced as that man's wife. Jane hoped the approval of their parents would ultimately sway Mary into changing her way of thinking, and that she would see, in time, that this deviation from the norm was for the best.

The family's only true consternation—to Mrs Bennet and the youngest girls, in particular—was their self-imposed seclusion at Longbourn. Mr Bennet had declared that until they received confirmation of Elizabeth's marriage, they should exercise great caution; no parties or outings meant no gossip. The more people who knew that Elizabeth had jilted one man at the altar and absconded with another, the more her reputation, and that of the entire family, would suffer. It was prudent to have proof of a union before encountering those outside of their family circle.

Jane felt that their friends and neighbours would be understanding, but she did realise that good people, upon occasion, spoke without consideration, and therefore suggested that her father confer with the servants and Mr Brown about maintaining secrecy. Hill, it seemed, had already imposed her mighty will upon the other servants. And Mr Brown actually applauded Elizabeth's escape, Mr Bennet had informed Jane with a chuckle. The rector was apparently no more fond of Mr Collins than the collective Bennets were, despite being a brother of the cloth. Family had been the only attendees of the failed wedding and the Gardiners and the Philipses promised to remain silent on the matter until Mr Bennet made a formal announcement. As for Mr Collins, he had left the area, thus the intelligence had yet to spread.

And so, despite the upheaval, all was surprisingly well at Longbourn.

Content to remain at home, Jane dutifully attended to her embroidery, though her mind wandered beyond the four walls of the sitting room. It travelled to Netherfield, where Charles should be preparing to ride to Longbourn. Then her thoughts travelled to wherever Mr Collins was, full of pity for his disappointment. It also travelled the road to Scotland to be with Elizabeth. Jane fervently prayed her sister was finding some measure of happiness as Mr Darcy's bride.

"This note just came for you, Miss Bennet."

"Thank you, Hill."

Jane accepted the note, and the scrawling, blotchy hand-writing across the front told her immediately whom it must be from. She experienced a moment of anxiety. Why should her betrothed be writing to her instead of coming himself? She broke the seal and read—or attempted to read—the contents.

Dearest Jane,

~~Appolo Apoli~~ Forgive me for not visiting as I promissed this morning, but my sisters arrived on my doorstep just as I was about to leave. Caroline has taken suddenly ill, nothing serious, and so I cannot attend you. You may still expect me for dinner.

Know that I ~~miss~~ adore you and shall be at your side as soon as may be. In the meantime, Darcy says that poetry is

the food of love and so I purused my library for some verse.
Darcy left this one behind...

Between the smears, cross-outs, and misspellings, Jane understood enough of Bingley's meaning to be placated. His words of affection were a balm to her disappointment. She was concerned for Miss Bingley, of course, but Jane was relieved she would still see her beloved later in the day. With a fluttering sigh, she pressed the single page to her heart and cast her gaze out the window. She would be patient.

CHAPTER SEVENTEEN

Never had Lady Catherine been so incensed as she was presently. She should have been, at that moment, sipping inferior tea in her sister's drawing room and dispensing advice to those who required it. Instead, she was trapped within the stifling confines of a carriage on a long journey with a simpering half-wit, all because her nephew Darcy had somehow got it into his head to marry for love. *What utter tripe.*

What would love ever bring him, pray? A short burst of happiness that would fade away to nothing within a year, if it even lasted beyond their misadventure. From what Lady Catherine knew of Collins and his connexions—and she knew it all—this Miss Elizabeth Bennet was as poor as she was unsuitable, absolutely nothing to Anne and Rosings. Whereas Miss Bennet had naught but her craftiness and the bloom of youth on her side, Anne was formed for Darcy in absolutely every respect.

Lady Catherine snorted with derision. To think she had once considered Darcy level-headed and intelligent. This sorry event proved him to be as susceptible to feminine charms as any other man. It ought to be impossible, whilst he still retained use of his reason, that her nephew should be so lost to infatuation as to make him forget what he owed to himself and his family, but she suspected that *reason* was not what had drawn him to that chit. A tolerably pretty face would not increase Pemberley's coffers, nor would it replace the distinction of marrying a woman of noble lineage, yet he seemed perfectly willing to throw Anne aside in order to slake his animal lusts. Were the shades of Pemberley to be thus polluted? Not if Lady Catherine had her say in the matter, and she was determined to have it, no matter the inconvenience to herself.

They were behind the wayward couple by a mere day. With much trepidation, the coachman had warned her that they might not catch up, and the fool footman agreed, but her ladyship was not one to abide failure. So long as they changed horses instead of resting them, did not make any unnecessary stops, and travelled overnight, they would make it in time to put an end to this farce. There was no other acceptable outcome.

Lady Catherine's narrow gaze snapped to Mr Collins when he let out an exceptionally loud snore. Her lip curled in disdain at the sight of him splayed across his bench with drool dripping from the corner of his mouth onto the lapel of his greatcoat.

Disgusting.

She had not forgot, much less forgiven, Collins's role in Darcy's elopement. Had the imbecile been more attentive to what was going on about him, he might have put a stop to this madness before it began. Darcy had snatched Miss Bennet from the very doorstep of the church where Collins himself was meant to marry her; he had been within yards of inter-vening and fallen flat on his face.

Worthless lump.

It had been mighty tempting to abandon him in London to find his own way back to Kent—in order to pack his bags and vacate the parsonage for a more worthy incumbent—but she had, at the last moment, discovered a new use for her bungling parson. He and his cousin would still be married, only over the anvil, thus removing the temptation of Miss Bennet from Darcy forever. After they were wed, Lady Catherine cared not what they did, but they would not be welcome back at Hunsford. Collins might hold the living there, but a whisper in his bishop's ear would see him stripped of the position. He would probably give it up readily if she commanded it of him.

With Miss Bennet allied elsewhere, Lady Catherine would have little trouble talking some sense into Darcy regarding Anne. They could still announce their engagement before the new year and be married in the spring, perhaps during his annual visit at Easter. Rosings was especially lovely that time of the year. Anne, too, was always in her best looks when the weather warmed, although she had a tendency to wilt in the heat of summer. Yes, April would do very well indeed.

Yet another undignified sound emerged from Collins, this one accompanied by a stench so overpowering that Lady Catherine was forced to bring her handkerchief to her nose. She should never have permitted him so many kippers at breakfast, and she certainly would disallow them entirely in future if this was the result. She kicked him viciously in the shin, and he awoke with an ignoble cry.

—————— ⚜ ——————

DARCY CHECKED HIS POCKET WATCH AS HE LOITERED IN THE inn's common room. The horses had been changed, their luncheon packed, and he was eager to get back on the road. They had been travelling all morning and had covered a good amount of road, but the leaden sky promised snow and he hoped to stay ahead of it. He only awaited his 'wife' to return from the necessary before they could depart.

Closing his eyes, Darcy reined in his ill temper. It was not Elizabeth's fault he was so testy today; that could be blamed on a sleepless night spent on a sofa too short for his tall frame. He might have ignored the discomfort and made do, as he had many a time in his university days after a night out with friends, but his lingering agitation over nearly taking Elizabeth on that same sofa, not to mention a deep yearning to feel her beneath him again, had kept him awake.

Elizabeth had magnanimously absolved him of guilt, but Darcy could not be entirely satisfied by her sweet pardon. Stealing a kiss would have been bad enough, but to pin her soft body beneath his and to ravish her mouth had been inexcusable. After all, Elizabeth did not love him—had not even been aware that Darcy was in love with her until two days ago —and such a precipitous leap in their intimacy must have distressed her. She claimed she was not offended, but how could she not be? This was not the way a gentleman behaved towards a lady whom he both loved and respected.

Worse, his conscience berated him for not feeling *more* remorse. Not all of his reflections were contrite. In fact, his final dream before waking had dwelt on what might have happened had he not stopped, imagining what it would have been like to slip Elizabeth's gown from her shoulders, taste her skin, and explore all the secrets of her form. He had jolted awake at half past four, feeling more uncomfortable and pained than even sleeping on an improper bed could account for. After that erotic vision, rest was impossible, so he quietly dressed and tiptoed out of the sitting room in search of coffee.

Unfortunately, said beverage had not erased his fatigue, and his exhausted mind persisted all morning in its preoccupation with bedding Elizabeth. Was his wedding night destined to be an awkward affair between two people who barely knew one another? There had been no hesitation the evening before, when exhaustion and maladroitness resulted in inflamed ardour, but would they become diffident with one another once they had sanction to know each other as husband and wife? There was also the decision of whether to pursue consummation immediately or wait until Elizabeth considered herself ready.

Just when Darcy felt his brain would burst from so much brooding, Elizabeth appeared, bundled up against the cold and ready to resume their journey.

"My apologies for taking so long. You seem impatient to resume our travels."

Yes, indeed, the sooner we reach Scotland, the better. Though his thoughts were restive, he hastily tucked his watch into his waistcoat pocket and demurred, "Not at all. Are you ready to go?"

Elizabeth's countenance lost some of its brilliancy as she continued to observe him. Quietly, she asked, "Are you well, Fitzwilliam? You still appear quite fatigued. Did you truly suffer on the sofa last night?"

A frisson blazed through Darcy's body at the thought of what he had *suffered* on that blasted piece of furniture. It was not at all what Elizabeth must be thinking. "I shall not say that I had an easy night," he said with forced lightness, "but I would have been more troubled had I taken the bed from you."

Elizabeth pressed her lips together and gave a slight nod. He grimaced inwardly, certain he had said the wrong thing again. Alas, there was nothing to be done about that now, so he simply proffered his arm and led her outside to where the carriage was waiting.

Darcy handed her into the forward-facing seat and took the one opposite. After he rapped on the roof, they were off.

"Will you not sit beside me?"

Darcy's eyes darted away from the window, where he had

determined to affix them for as long as possible, and looked to Elizabeth. Her expression was bemused, perhaps a touch wounded, as she patted the seat next to her. Oh, how he wished to oblige her—but he should not whilst his feelings were in such conflict and hers remained a mystery. So he merely said, "I thought you might prefer more room to stretch out today."

"I see."

Now she appeared disappointed. *Blast! Should I deny her?* Darcy's body moved practically of its own accord, already attuned to his beloved's every whim, and settled beside her. The radiance of her good cheer was restored as she tucked a travelling rug round them both. He did his utmost to calm his body's reaction to her proximity when she leant across him to spread their covering more equitably, but with her scent in his nose and her torso all but pressed into his, it was a losing battle. Thankfully, she withdrew without apparently noticing his…discomfort.

"There now," Elizabeth declared as she settled into the natural nook between his shoulder and hip. "You must take this opportunity to nap. Do not fret for me, as I have a book to keep me well entertained until our next stop."

Darcy grumbled a vague sort of agreement, knowing that any repose would be impossible with Elizabeth curled up against him. He would be fortunate if this interlude did not disturb his slumber tonight! Perhaps a bit of careful distance was necessary, if only to preserve his sanity. However, her warmth and the rhythm of the carriage quickly lulled him into a deep sleep.

CHAPTER EIGHTEEN

Several days later

Elizabeth sighed and withdrew from the window. The snow that they had managed to stay ahead of for the better part of a week had at last caught up with them, forcing them to stop a mere dozen miles or so from the border. It had not abated one whit since they had arrived at the inn and, in fact, fell more heavily than ever. There was little chance of their getting back on the road tomorrow, much less that day. They were decidedly trapped until the weather improved.

She jumped when the door of the private dining room abruptly opened and Darcy strode through, looking grim.

"They have only one room available."

"Oh. With only one bed, I presume?"

"You presume correctly."

Darcy paced away from her to look out the window, standing almost exactly where she had been moments before. His countenance declared him to be as dissatisfied with the weather as she, perhaps more so. "We shall have to remain here at least until the morrow. As that is Christmas Eve, I suppose we must prepare ourselves to remain some days longer. We shall be lucky to make it to Pemberley by the new year."

Elizabeth moved closer, her hand outstretched to rest upon his shoulder, but remembered herself and withdrew it. Ever since their regrettably impulsive moment of passion, excepting a few hours when she had all but begged him to sit beside her in the carriage, Darcy had flinched from her touch. She pretended not to notice, but could not lie to herself. It hurt. She would never wish to make him uncomfortable, and so she had abstained from physical contact as much as possible.

"That is, indeed, regrettable," she finally replied, "but we can count ourselves fortunate to be comfortably ensconced here. We might be much worse off."

The Red Hare was commendably clean, there was tolerable food, as confirmed by their luncheon, and the furnishings were exceptionally well maintained, nary a scratch or threadbare cushion to be seen. Had they been stuck in one of the more rustic hamlets they had passed earlier in the day, their lodgings might not be so pleasant. But here they were, scant miles from the border.

Darcy did not remove his eyes from the whitening scene outside. "I suppose."

Elizabeth felt a pang at his curt dismissal. Was the

prospect of sharing such close quarters with her truly so abhorrent as to blacken his mood? His odd behaviour the morning following his night on the sofa, and his heightened consciousness of her touch since, made her worry that the intimacy of a shared bedchamber was distressing to him. In her more anxious moments, Elizabeth wondered what that might portend for their marriage. Darcy continued to be amiable in other ways—using her Christian name, seeing to her every need and desire, openly discussing a wide range of topics— but for the past few days, he had not instigated contact with her other than to take her hand when ascending or descending the carriage steps. She waited for him to resume his former habit of brushing his fingertips against hers and guiding her gently with his hand against her lower back, yet he resolutely kept his distance. *Is he already regretting his rash decision to elope?*

But how could that possibly be? Darcy had been most eager to reach Scotland for the past week, expressing not the slightest desire to turn back. Even if he were attempting to hide his discontent, Elizabeth had come to understand him so well as of late and felt certain she would have seen some sign of it. Indeed, just that morning he had exhibited a charming, boyish sort of giddiness at the possibility of being married by dinner time. His withdrawal was as perplexing as it was painful.

Perhaps he is merely frustrated by the circumstances. I must not imagine the worst! Have I learnt nothing from my previous misjudgments?

Exhaling much of her anxiety in a sigh, Elizabeth did her

best to soothe Darcy's ruffled temper. "I know you are disappointed to be stranded here, especially so close to our destination, but let us think of our situation only as it gives us pleasure. We are safe, warm, and in excellent company. I could not ask for more."

When Darcy pivoted to face her, Elizabeth noted, with much relief, a smile softening his countenance. "You are perfectly right. Forgive me for being churlish."

Again, Elizabeth was tempted to reach for him. Again, she suppressed the impulse. "There is nothing to forgive. I am as disappointed as you. We might have been married today were it not for the bad luck of a snowstorm."

"And yet, you have not exacted your ill temper upon me as I have you. I shall begin following your lead and behave in a more genteel manner."

A knock sounded at the door, and the innkeeper informed them their room was ready. Darcy winced almost imperceptibly at this news, and Elizabeth feared he was gritting his teeth. *Alas, this promises to be a most awkward night.*

With a sweep of his arm that indicated she should precede him, Darcy followed Elizabeth out and up the stairs. So attuned was she to his presence by now that she knew he followed her from a distance of at least three paces.

Their accommodation consisted of a bedroom and a separate sitting room. Both were as comfortable and clean as the rest of the establishment, but there was one significant drawback.

"You cannot possibly sleep on *that*," Elizabeth declared the moment they were alone.

Darcy looked to the sofa that she indicated with an accusing finger and shrugged his shoulders with indifference. The taut set of his mouth, however, gave away his displeasure. "There is little choice. I shall make do."

Elizabeth scoffed. If the sofa at that previous inn had been a trial for Darcy and his tall frame, this one would be torturous. It was so short, she doubted that two adults could sit upon it without touching one another, and its spindly legs looked barely able to hold a grown man's weight.

She said, "I doubt that *I* could sleep on it, and I am far slighter than you. The bed would be much more comfortable—"

"I could never—"

"—for us both."

Darcy transferred his glower from the offending sofa to her. "Out of the question."

"Fitzwilliam, do be reasonable," Elizabeth exclaimed in exasperation. "You cannot spend even a single night on that tiny thing. The bed is plenty large enough for two, and I am more than willing to share."

A deep flush rose up from beneath Darcy's collar and flooded his face, making him nearly the same colour as the claret they had partaken of at dinner the previous evening. The heat in her own cheeks indicated to Elizabeth that she must look much the same, but she could not, would not, retract her invitation. They were on the precipice of wedlock—might even have been exchanging vows that afternoon had the weather not prevented them—and it was ridiculous for either of them to suffer under the circumstances.

So she added, "Just because we share a bed does not mean that we must…"

Memories flooded into Elizabeth's mind of Darcy's lips hovering just above hers, the feel of his tongue plundering her mouth, his exquisite weight moving against her body. Her breath hitched and she found herself unable to finish her thought.

Darcy regarded her warily but said nothing.

Pushing her mortification aside, Elizabeth cleared her throat and continued, "Regardless, I cannot abide leaving you in so much discomfort when I might prevent it. I have every faith in our mutual restraint, if that is your primary concern."

He swallowed, opened his mouth, and then closed it again. After another moment of struggle, he said formally, "I thank you for your concern, madam, but I shall be more at ease here. Should the sofa prove too disagreeable, there is always the floor."

There was nothing else to say on the matter if he felt so strongly as to repeatedly rebuff her. *Very well! If he insists upon being stubborn, I shall leave him to it. Let him be stiff and uncomfortable!*

Elizabeth raised her chin, muttered a quick excuse, and stalked into the much contested bedchamber to calm her temper. She would be better able to speak to Darcy again with equanimity if allowed half an hour to herself.

As the carriage gave another jolting shudder, Collins clamped his eyes shut and prayed for his life. The weather outside was abysmal, a composition of sleet and snow that hammered against the walls of Lady Catherine's coach, while gale forces threatened to overturn them at any moment.

They should have stopped at the last village they passed through, but her ladyship had insisted the coachman continue without so much as pausing for a warm drink. They would have to change the horses soon, lest they lame one and be stranded in the countryside in the middle of a snowstorm, but her ladyship was resolute about travelling through the night, as they had so far. Not once had she deigned to allow them a night's rest in an actual bed, determined as she was to hunt down the wayward couple. So uncomfortable was Collins that he longed even for the dubious comfort of damp sheets and crawling bugs.

"Do cease your muttering!" Lady Catherine commanded sharply.

Collins immediately halted his supplications and lowered his folded hands onto his lap. "Forgive me, ma'am, I was merely praying for our continued safety and—"

"I know what you were doing, and you can stop it this instant! It is as though you believe we are in some danger, and I cannot comprehend why. It is just a bit of snow and wind, and we shall navigate it without injury or mishap. I have the best coachman in all of England, not to mention the sturdiest carriage. You worry over nothing."

The wind howled so loudly as to make the last part of Lady Catherine's statement nearly unintelligible.

"B-but should we not stop soon and allow the storm to pass? The cold is severe, we cannot travel quickly—"

"We shall stop at Gretna Green and not before! Really, Mr Collins, we are chasing after *your* betrothed, a strumpet who has ensnared my dear nephew. Considering your complaints, I begin to wonder whether you truly wish to recover them at all. Is this your gratitude for my patronage? Is nothing due to me on that score?"

"Yes! That is, no! I-I mean, of course I am eminently obliged to your ladyship for your condescension, your generosity, your most excellent advice in all matters great and small, but I am concerned—not that I doubt your exceptional judgment, you understand—that we might face some calamity should we not get out of this weather. If this carriage were overturned, or we found ourselves stranded far from civilisation, then we would never catch up with them."

Lady Catherine peered at him, her mouth set in a firm and unforgiving line. Collins experienced a small thrill at the prospect of the great Lady Catherine de Bourgh considering his counsel and bowing to his wisdom.

"We press on."

Collins cowered more deeply into his seat and resumed his prayers—silently this time.

CHAPTER NINETEEN

A sharp pain in his lower back was what officially woke Darcy, but to say he had been properly asleep would have been disingenuous. He had drifted in and out of wakefulness for hours as cold and stiffness seeped into his body. The blasted sofa loomed beside him from where he reposed upon the hard floor—the more comfortable choice —and taunted him with its worthlessness. *I would chop it up into firewood had I an axe with which to do it. Then, perhaps, it might serve a purpose.*

Darcy rose to a sitting position, wincing at every pop and creak of his protesting joints, and looked to the window. It was still dark, probably well before dawn, but the pile of brilliant white snow accumulated on the sill portended another day of travel lost. Instead of grumbling and going back to sleep again, a prospect that held minimal appeal, Darcy decided to get up and dress for the day. He did so quickly, having removed only his shoes, jacket, and waistcoat the night before, and stepped closer to the window for a more thorough inspection of the inn's courtyard.

The moon above was just bright enough to illuminate the pristine whiteness that covered the landscape, all other objects appearing starkly black by comparison. This view confirmed it: they would not leave The Red Hare today.

Resting his forehead against the frigid glass, Darcy attempted to rein in his disappointment. They were so close to the border as to be maddening; another three or four hours in the carriage and they would cross into Scotland. Unfortunately, no equipage, save perhaps a sleigh, could traverse so much as a mile in the current conditions, so there was nothing for it. If they were fortunate, the roads would be cleared enough in a day or so, but today was Christmas Eve, and that created its own challenges.

Darcy moved away from the window before he became unreasonably chilled and resumed his spot on the floor, refusing to sit on the horrid sofa. Wrapping himself in his blanket, he stared vacantly at the dying fire as his mind reviewed his sorry predicament.

One, he would not be married by Christmas as he had hoped.

Two, his dearest, loveliest Elizabeth was cross with him.

And three, he was beset by powerful temptations—that of Elizabeth and a large bed.

The first complication simply could not be helped; no one was in control of the forces of nature, regardless of their influence in the world of man. Darcy could have more cheerfully

suffered the disappointment of delay had it not been for diffi-
culties two and three. Without the benefit of marriage, he was
wary of sharing a bed with Elizabeth, yet she was obviously
offended by his refusal. She could not know how her glances,
touches, and scent tormented and tempted him; it was sweet
agony to be in such close quarters with her. He might have
risked it and damned the consequences—what could it truly
hurt, so close to their ultimate destination—but so long as he
remained unsure of her feelings for him, it was best to maintain a careful distance.

If her exasperation with him was any indication, Elizabeth
was neither so affected by him—which, in and of itself, was
another provocation—nor aware of how mightily he struggled.
Darcy had forced himself to abstain from so much as touching
her, lest he give in to his baser desires and kiss her senseless.
Given her previous response to his ardour, Darcy thought she
might not be disinclined, but then that only made the temptation stronger.

Darcy sighed and tipped his head back to rest upon the
hard seat of the sofa. If only Elizabeth knew how desperately
he wanted to storm into her bedchamber and join her there.
But to avoid dishonouring them both, he must maintain his
distance until they were properly wed. Then and only then
would he share a bed with her—assuming she wished to be his
wife in that way.

And if she did not...well, after saying their vows, he
would simply bide his time. Pemberley was large, the
mistress was afforded her own apartment, and he could more
easily, if not happily, grant her the space and time she

required to become accustomed to the idea of consummating their union.

Assuming they were afforded such a luxury of choice. If any party contested the validity of their marriage, Darcy might have to convince Elizabeth to lie with him at least once to protect them against an annulment. She would see the sense in it, he was sure, but this was hardly the manner in which Darcy hoped to join with her for the first time. Or at any other time, for that matter. He wished for Elizabeth to come to him out of love, not duty or necessity. But what alternative did they have? He would not leave their union vulnerable to dissolution. He would not allow anyone to take her from him.

But how was he to convey this intention? It was a conversation which must occur but would be exceedingly awkward to instigate. *Dearest, loveliest Elizabeth, I know you do not yet love me, in spite of already being my wife, but I hope you might allow me the privilege of a husband just once in case your loathsome cousin or my meddlesome aunt attempts to invalidate our marriage. After that, I am at your disposal whenever you should choose it.*

It was a topic somehow both too personal and *im*personal, one that transfigured the most intimate aspect of their married lives into a business transaction. Darcy was not anticipating this uncomfortable discussion with any measure of delight. Perhaps he might delay it until it became absolutely necessary. He groaned.

A sharp creak and the muffled rustle of fabric stilled his heart momentarily; there was stirring from within Elizabeth's bedchamber. He waited and listened carefully for an interminably long minute, but it was again quiet. No doubt she had merely shifted in her sleep.

Darcy looked to the window once more to see a weak light filtering through the gloom of an overcast sky. Not wishing to encounter Elizabeth's knowing gaze when she found him on the floor, he determined that he would seek his coffee downstairs in the common room, and perhaps break his fast as well. He would have a tray sent up to Elizabeth while he was at it.

So decided, Darcy quickly untangled himself from his blanket and silently exited the room.

CHAPTER TWENTY

T hough a book lay open upon her lap, Elizabeth had paid it no heed for at least a quarter of an hour. The pages remained unturned as she watched the flames dance merrily in the fireplace, distracted by her own melancholy thoughts.

It was Christmas Eve, and she was homesick. Instead of sitting down to table with her family and half the neighbourhood for a holiday feast, she was stranded in a tiny inn, far from everyone and everything she had ever known, and with a man who seemed nearly as discontent to be there as she. It was a miserable way to spend what should be a festive evening.

When Elizabeth had awoken that morning, the sitting room had been empty and very cold. Instead of breakfasting with her betrothed, as she had come to expect over the course of their journey, Darcy had absented himself—to the common room, she assumed—and sent up a tray for her to eat by herself. Not an auspicious beginning to the day.

When he returned, Darcy had apologised for his neglect, which was much to his credit, but then proceeded to settle himself across the sitting room from her for the rest of the day. Whilst Elizabeth contented herself with the hard sofa—*how did he manage to sleep on it?*—Darcy sat at the table, well out of reach, ostensibly reading a book. He occasionally remarked on the still-dismal weather or made enquiries as to her comfort. Though it was reassuring to know he had not forgotten her entirely, Elizabeth was hard pressed to offer anything in return other than stilted responses.

She fought against being vexed with him, truly, but Darcy had returned to being that aloof, haughty gentleman she first met at the Meryton assembly in October. Were they not presently stranded at an inn just a few hours from Gretna Green, Elizabeth might have convinced herself that she had imagined his regard for her and dreamt their flight from Hertfordshire. In the absence of his more amiable behaviour, it all seemed so fanciful.

Checking the time on the mantel clock, Elizabeth sighed. Her mother would be presenting the flaming plum pudding about now. Elizabeth wondered whether Jane would find the ring in her slice this year, thus doubly ensuring her marriage to Mr Bingley. With amusement, Elizabeth recalled that she had got it last year, and the token had proved prophetic. She was hardly superstitious, but it was a diverting coincidence all the same.

"Are you well, my dear?"

Elizabeth looked up, astonished to find Darcy standing immediately before her. His face was drawn into an expression of concern as he gazed down upon her. It occurred to Elizabeth in a flash of annoyance that this was the closest he had come to her all day.

Suppressing her pique, Elizabeth replied, "I am well, only missing home. On Christmas Eve, my mother invites the principal families of Meryton to Longbourn, and it is the highlight of the festive season for us. The party is always noisy and overwarm, but it is my favourite night of the year, with so many of my loved ones round me."

Darcy's countenance took on a woeful shade. "And this year you must content yourself with only my company. I am hardly equal to a houseful of family and friends."

Endeared by this sombre observation and ashamed that her ungenerous musings had pained him, Elizabeth countered, "I do not agree. It is the quality of companionship which matters most, not the quantity. I might miss my family, but it does not necessarily follow that you are in any way lacking."

"If you say so." In spite of his quiet demurral, Darcy's countenance lightened enough to allow a slight upturn of his lips.

"Come," Elizabeth said, suddenly inspired, "sit next to me." She shifted to one side of the dreadful sofa and patted the cushion next to her for emphasis.

Any ease in Darcy's aspect immediately fled. "I would not wish to crowd you."

Prickled again by annoyance, she insisted. "Sit."

He looked as if he wished to argue, but capitulated instead.

He seated himself as far away as the sofa would allow—which was not very, perhaps two inches—and did his utmost to avoid contact with her. Elizabeth was tempted to sigh again but allowed him his way.

"Tell me about Pemberley's Christmas traditions," she asked. Darcy could always be tempted to discuss his home, and it was her hope that the topic might bring back the affability he had expressed several days ago.

He took a breath—a good sign for a suitably verbose response, she thought. "As we are a small family, just my sister and me, our celebrations are meagre compared to yours. We light a yule log, of course, and arrange baskets to give our tenants on St Stephen's Day, but otherwise we spend the day in quiet reflection."

"Much as we have today?"

"Very like."

Well, that was something of a relief. Perhaps it was not Elizabeth's presence that had sent Darcy into reticent stillness; it was merely his way at Christmas.

"Do you exchange gifts?"

"Small ones. Last year, my sister embroidered some handkerchiefs for my use. Here." He fumbled to withdraw a square of linen from his jacket pocket, colouring and apologising when his elbow accidentally brushed against her arm. "She does excellent work."

"Indeed." Elizabeth smiled at the raised 'FD' surrounded by small clusters of Sweet Williams. The stitches were uneven and pulled tight in places, causing the cloth to pucker, but she could not have done much better herself. Regardless of the actual skill involved, she was charmed by how proudly Darcy presented the embroidery to her notice. He was obviously a doting brother to Miss Darcy.

Elizabeth handed it back to him. "I hope you are as satisfied with my paltry attempts in future years. I am perhaps better at stitching than I am at playing the pianoforte, but that is not much recommendation."

Darcy chuckled as he returned the handkerchief to his pocket. "I cannot imagine that I shall be displeased with anything you have to offer me."

She bit back a remark about how her touch had become distasteful of late, not wishing to spoil their companionable moment.

He added, "Perhaps we might invite your family to Pemberley next Christmas, or go to Longbourn if your mother does not wish to give up her duties as hostess. Aside from Georgiana, I generally spend the holiday alone, and it might be a fine change to be part of a merry party."

Elizabeth could not help but regard him sceptically, knowing as she did his true opinion of her mother and younger sisters, to say nothing of her relations in trade and crowds in general. His inflection and mien were both sincere, however, so she belatedly accepted that he meant what he said.

"Would my aunt and uncle from London also be included in the invitation? It is their tradition to join us at Christmas."

She thought she detected a twitch at the corner of his eye, but he replied with admirable equanimity. "Of course."

Though she suspected that Darcy continued to hold reservations over maintaining a connexion to the Gardiners, Elizabeth bestowed upon him a genuine smile. That he still hesitated to overcome his prejudice only made his willingness to please her more valuable. She experienced a surge of affection for him so strong that she could not help but to move closer and embrace him. "Thank you."

But before her arms could close round him, Darcy leapt up from the sofa and scurried away. Elizabeth at first was astonished, then hurt, and finally furious as she observed how he nonchalantly rested his forearm against the mantelpiece with his back to her. When he spoke, it was with a perfect composure that she could not share. "'Tis nothing."

"So, my touch is now disgusting to you, is it?" The accusation flew from Elizabeth's mouth before she could make the attempt to suppress it.

Darcy turned quickly to face her, aghast. "Of course not!"

"Then why do you flee from me every time I come close?"

"I…Elizabeth, you do not understand—"

"No, I do *not* understand!" she cried, standing but moving no closer. She clenched her hands as she fought to rein in her temper. "You claim that you were not put off by…by my *forwardness* a few days ago, but you have since treated me like I carry some ghastly disease! In my darker moments, I wonder whether you already regret asking me to marry you, if you can no longer abide my touch."

Darcy rushed forward and, without the hesitation he had displayed of late, clasped both of her hands within his. "Forgive me, my love. I did not mean to give you that impression. I abstain from your touch for exactly the opposite reason. My passion for you is so strong as to dissolve all my self-control, and I would not wish to impose any…affections upon you until we are wed and you are ready for them."

Elizabeth huffed and resisted the impulse to roll her eyes. "I have not once felt imposed upon. You know enough of my frankness to believe me when I say that I would have informed you of such had it occurred."

"I do, but it is hardly so simple."

Darcy's voice and countenance were both plaintive, but Elizabeth would not be so easily swayed.

"Then explain it to me," she demanded. "You apparently have enough restraint to avoid contact with me altogether, but not enough to resist imposing your *affections* upon me? I cannot see how one is more difficult than the other."

Darcy sighed and released one of her hands to rake his fingers through his hair. "I cannot explain it other than to say that you are a great temptation to me, one that I might be inclined to partake of with the slightest encouragement from you."

Elizabeth clenched her teeth so tightly together that they squeaked. "So it is *my* fault?"

"No! That is not my meaning."

"It is what you said. I am apparently so *tempting* as to render you as witless as a rutting beast! No, you cannot *possibly* come near me lest you throw me down and have your way with me."

"That is ridiculous!"

"I agree!" Elizabeth was almost shouting in Darcy's face, but given the astonished expression upon it, she felt she had made her point. More calmly, she said, "Regardless of the temptation we *both* face, you forget that we can still exercise our free will. I am safe with you, I know it, and I wish you could trust yourself as much as I do."

"It is difficult," he admitted with much apparent frustration. "As much as I wish to be with you in all ways—and I would have to be made of stone not to desire you—I feel I cannot allow myself the privilege when we are not, as yet, man and wife."

"You realise we shall be married in a matter of days, do you not? That we might already be married were it not for the poor weather?"

"It has occurred to me once or twice, yes," Darcy replied drily, nearly causing Elizabeth to laugh in the midst of their otherwise serious conversation. "However, we are *not* yet married, and thus it behoves us to be cautious."

"Even were we to give in to our baser urges—and I am not inclined to think we would against our better judgments—it cannot matter much at this point. My reputation is irreparably compromised by our elopement, and many would assume that we have already anticipated our vows, regardless of the truth. You need not cling so tightly to your self-control."

Darcy swallowed and lowered his head. "It is less about the practicalities of our situation or what others might think, and more related to…how you feel about me."

Taken aback, Elizabeth's mouth fell open. "How so?"

"I said before that I did not wish to importune you with my advances, and that is the truth. However," Darcy sighed and tunnelled his fingers through his hair again, "what I left unsaid was that I would prefer to wait until I am assured of your love before we…before you accept me completely as your husband. This might be impractical, considering the, um, irregular nature of our marriage, but I would not for the world want to take such liberties without knowing you felt for me as I do for you."

Darcy's gaze rose, tentatively, to connect with hers.

Elizabeth felt bashful all of a sudden. There was such vulnerability in the depths of his eyes. What should she say? Her feelings…she could not put a name to them, but they were vastly different from what they were before. That she was fond of him and attracted to him was not a question, but did she experience anything more fervid? Could she say she was in love with him? She bit her lower lip, unsure.

Glancing away, she gave Darcy the only answer she could relate with tolerable honesty. It was fumbling and somewhat incoherent, which was perhaps the best reflection of her true feelings. "I…I care for you, deeply, but as yet I cannot say… that is, I am well on my way to…"

Elizabeth felt the gentle nudge of a finger urging her chin upwards, and she followed its persuasion. Darcy's countenance was solemn—crestfallen, even—and Elizabeth's heart clenched painfully. "Do not make yourself uneasy, my love," he murmured. "I daresay it was too much to hope for so soon."

So saying, Darcy pressed a gentle kiss to Elizabeth's forehead and stepped back. Choked on her own emotions, Elizabeth bid him a strangled goodnight and fled into the bedchamber.

CHAPTER TWENTY-ONE

Elizabeth tipped her face up to the grey, overcast sky, seeking warmth but finding none. All she felt was cold, a chill that wrapped round her like a wet woollen blanket and weighed her down in the encroaching darkness. Her breath, which customarily would have risen about her in a plume, was lacking the necessary heat to make itself visible. Was she breathing at all? She was frozen from the inside out—unable to move, unable to perceive any other sensation, aware only of how alone she was.

"Elizabeth."

There! A fleeting blaze of heat across the back of her neck. Elizabeth struggled to turn, but it was impossible; the cold would not release her. It was as if she were sculpted out of ice, unbending and brittle.

"*Elizabeth.*"

That same delicious heat prickled across her skin and

thawed her. She moved; her heart began thudding a slow tempo within her chest.

"Elizabeth, look at me."

"F-Fitzwilliam...?" Elizabeth's lips trembled to form his name.

"Do you love me?"

A searing fever rushed through Elizabeth's body, and she gasped at the intensity of it. The ice, that horrible cold, melted away, and she was freed, liberated by the fire that overwhelmed her, burned her, frightened her with its sudden and unexpected ferocity. Elizabeth collapsed onto the ground, exhausted and shaking.

"Do not make yourself uneasy, my love. I daresay it was too much to hope for so soon..." Darcy's dear voice faded to a despondent whisper, and his warmth likewise dissolved into nothing, leaving behind only the cold.

"Wait!" Elizabeth cried, struggling to turn and search for him, but her joints stiffened and hardened her in place. "Fitzwilliam, come back! I do love—"

A dark, lumpy shadow rose up in front of her, blocking any attempt she might make to locate him. The outline took on a familiar, sinister shape, and its eyes glinted possessively. "There you are. I have been looking for you, Wife."

Mr Collins lunged for her, and Elizabeth used the last ounce of her free will to scream.

"Elizabeth! Elizabeth, calm yourself! Can you hear me?"

The sharp relief of reality imposed itself upon Elizabeth's mind, and the menacing spectre of Mr Collins evanesced like a puff of tobacco smoke: acrid, disagreeable, and lingering, but essentially gone. She was secure and warm; there were no jilted spectres waiting to drag her into a miserable existence. She was with Darcy, and he would protect her.

Fitzwilliam! Elizabeth stiffened as she recognised the weight of his arms round her, the scent of his skin as he pressed her to his shoulder. He must have heard her scream and come to her aid.

"Shh, all is well," Darcy murmured against her temple, rocking them both back and forth in a gentle motion. "You are safe, my love. Nothing can hurt you."

Elizabeth relaxed more deeply into his embrace and exhaled a shuddering breath. Tears began to form, so she pressed her face into the welcoming warmth of his chest. She clutched what material she could within her grasping fingers, noting muzzily that his cravat and waistcoat were missing. It must be late; he was never so improperly attired before bed.

He cradled her in his lap, shushing and mumbling endearments as she shivered and wept. At length, Elizabeth calmed and her tears ceased, yet she made no move to pull away. Perhaps it was due to her awful dream, but she feared what might happen if she let him go.

"Was your dream very terrible?"

Darcy's whispered enquiry tickled the top of her head. She simply nodded.

"Would you like to speak of it?"

She swallowed against the lump in her throat. "It…it was awful. I was so cold and…and my coldness chased you away. Then Mr Collins…came for me." She shuddered at the memory of the parson's claw-like fingers grabbing for her, intent on dragging her away with him.

Darcy's arms tightened round her, and he leant back against the headboard. "Nothing could chase me away from you, nothing at all. You need never fear it."

Elizabeth pulled back just enough to look at him. A fresh welling of tears stung her eyes, and the droplets scattered as she attempted to blink them back into submission. "And yet I ran from you earlier. I do not deserve such steadfast devotion when I am frightened away by my own feelings."

Light from the dying fire lit Darcy's face, and she noted a slight flinch before he replied. "You must not be so hard on yourself. It is not fair to expect you to feel as strongly for me as I do for you at this juncture. After all, it has been scarcely a week since you began thinking of me as your future husband. If anything, it is I who has been unreasonable, asking you if…" His words trailed off, much like they had in Elizabeth's awful vision, as if carried away by an ill wind.

Elizabeth shook her head frantically. "No, you do not understand. I did not run from your feelings for me, but rather my own. I…" She sucked in a deep breath, pushing down the trepidation that urged her to leave her sentiments unspoken. "I love you."

Darcy stared at her, his expression one of shock, wonder, and disbelief. "You…what?"

"I *love* you," she repeated, this time with more fervency. "I cannot say it came on gradually, for honestly it has struck me with all the force of a runaway carriage, but it is true nonetheless: I am in love with you."

"Elizabeth, you need not—"

She sat up and away from him, but kept her hand pressed to his heart. She could feel it beating rapidly beneath her palm. "I do not say this to flatter you, or—or to express my gratitude for all you have done for me, but because it is the truth. It is so true that I have frightened myself with it! Ordinarily, my courage rises at every unexpected circumstance, but my love for you came on so suddenly and so powerfully that I knew not how to accept it. And so I fled."

Darcy raised his hand to cup her cheek, and she felt the tremble in his fingers. "Are you certain?"

"As certain as I am that you are the only man in the world I could ever be prevailed upon to marry."

With an inarticulate cry, Darcy used the hand caressing her face to pull her closer, and their mouths crashed together. Though their previous kiss had hardly been tentative or soft, this one somehow managed to be yet more potent. The way he devoured her…Elizabeth had never experienced the like before, never could have fathomed it. It was all she could do to clasp him tightly to her and respond with encouraging fervour.

After several feverish minutes locked in passionate embrace, they broke apart, panting as if they had just sprinted up a hill. Elizabeth was surprised to find herself upon her back, one knee bent upward and the hem of her nightgown bunched up to her hips. Darcy's hand was cupped along the length of her exposed thigh, it having apparently encouraged her current state of undress.

"For…forgive me. I forgot myself," Darcy wheezed, out of breath. He lifted his weight from her, but did not withdraw entirely, for which Elizabeth was grateful. She did not wish to be abandoned to the chill of the room as in her dream.

She brushed an errant lock of hair from his forehead with a soft smile. "No more than I. And look, you restrained yourself."

"Barely."

"Yet you did. See? My trust in you is not misplaced."

Darcy pointedly drew the fabric of her nightgown down the length of her leg, covering the flesh he had exposed in the haze of his passion. Elizabeth could do naught but giggle at the severe look he levelled at her as he did so.

"All the same," he said, "I should leave you now before my resolve is tested further."

"No!" Amusement fled and panic took its place as Elizabeth threw her arms round Darcy's neck and clutched him to her. "Do not leave! Stay with me."

"Elizabeth, I cannot…"

"Please?"

Darcy gave a soft sigh, and any resistance remaining within him seemed to evaporate. Tension left his body, and he relaxed into her embrace once more. "I can deny you nothing, my love. I only hope that you have no cause to repine in the morning."

Elizabeth gave him a brief but fierce kiss. "I shall never

repine any intimacy with you, regardless of what form it takes. I am ready to be your wife in all ways."

Darcy's eyes widened, and Elizabeth thought she discerned a slight increase in the tempo of his breathing. "You will not regret…?"

Weary of attempting to explain her desires, Elizabeth placed her lips against his, more softly than ever before. She lingered there, questioning, until Darcy responded in kind, his mouth moving in rhythm to hers. His warm, wonderful weight descended upon Elizabeth anew, and she sighed with satisfaction.

From there, words became unnecessary. It was far more efficacious—and most gratifying—to show him how she felt.

CHAPTER TWENTY-TWO

A s the sun rose on Christmas morning, its rosy beam crept through the window and bathed Elizabeth's slumbering face in a warm glow. Darcy observed the light's progression across the counterpane, up the undulating curves of her form, and over the delicate crests of her chin and nose. Any moment now, it would tickle at the fringe of her eyelashes and she would stir, opening her magnificent eyes, but he was content to wait and look his fill in the meantime.

Beneath the covers, neither of them worn a stitch of clothing, proof that last night had not been another erotic dream. The most responsible part of him, one that continued to slumber on this drowsy morn, would eventually browbeat him for having taken the liberties of a husband with Elizabeth before they were properly wed. But Darcy was still so awash in bliss that he assumed he would not feel the requisite guilt until much later.

At least part of his conscience was assuaged by the knowledge that Elizabeth loved him. She *loved* him. Perhaps it was this revelation of her attachment, bestowed upon him with sincerity, as much as his profound satisfaction that kept self-admonition at bay. It mattered not; for the nonce, he would watch Elizabeth, his wife now in all ways save legalities, as she slept.

And truly, she was enchanting in repose. Elizabeth was never entirely tame, always charmingly unrestrained in some small way, but she was positively wild now. Her unbound curls seemed to have increased in both volume and ferocity, fluffed out from her head like a lion's mane. Her mouth hung slightly open and, most endearingly of all, she snored lightly, almost inaudibly—the occasional little snort or snuffle whenever she moved. Most ladies would be horrified to be seen thusly, but then, none of them could possibly be as captivating as his Elizabeth.

One loose, feathery coil of hair fell across her eye when she burrowed more deeply into their shared covers. Darcy, who had admirably restrained himself from touching her since waking nearly half an hour ago, tucked it behind her ear. The tickle of his fingertips must have roused her, for an instant later she gave a small twitch and a delectable moan, and further retreated into her pillow. Then, as though the sun was rising again, she opened her eyes and smiled. "Good morning."

"Good morning, my love." Darcy's voice emerged as a rumble. "How did you sleep?"

"As well as can be expected," she quipped. "And yourself?"

"Better than I have in years."

Elizabeth turned more fully onto her side and winced. Darcy's contentment waned when he considered the possible cause. "Are you…well?"

"Am I well?"

"That is, are you…sore?" In spite of the intimacies they had partaken of only hours before, Darcy blushed at his suggestion.

Elizabeth appeared sweetly confused a moment longer before comprehension dawned in her eyes. "Oh! No, not at all —or at least, not much. I was merely wincing at a slight ache in my neck."

Palpable relief flowed into Darcy, and he drew Elizabeth closer, his lips skimming her exposed shoulder. He delighted in the resulting shiver. "Is there anything I might provide for your present relief, madam?"

"Mm…perhaps a little attention to where it hurts would be in order." Elizabeth coyly tilted her head and stretched out her throat for his inspection. She bit her lip as if forcing back some secret diversion.

"You mean here?" Darcy nibbled his way up from the crest of her shoulder to the valley where it met her neck.

Elizabeth's breath hitched and her fingers found their way into his hair, holding him in place. "Yes, just there."

It was some time before either of them proposed getting out of bed.

IT WAS MORE THAN A DAY LATER THAT THE ANTICIPATED remorse began to creep in to disturb Darcy's comfort.

They spent Christmas Day in a state of bliss, trading kisses and musing on how their families might be celebrating without them, and there had been no room at all for regret. That evening, when Elizabeth invited Darcy into her bed, there had been naught in his mind or heart but becoming one with her again. They had explored and teased one another well into the night before falling into untroubled sleep, then did so again in the early hours of the morning. Darcy had never been so well sated in his life, nor so content. During that short time, there was nothing else in the entire world save for him and Elizabeth, no duty or technicality to dampen their ardour.

Guilt struck that afternoon when Darcy ventured outside to determine the state of the roads. Without Elizabeth by his side, it was more difficult to reconcile having seduced her before their wedding night. One time might have been forgiven, but they had repeatedly and willingly transgressed. There was nothing for it now, of course, but his stomach soured when he thought of how careless he had been.

When he re-entered their rooms, Elizabeth closed her book and looked up, cheerful and unbothered by any gloomy thoughts. "How does it look? Shall we be able to leave tomorrow, do you think?"

He evaded her gaze and went directly to the fireplace, where he turned his back to her under the guise of warming his hands. "Yes, indeed. Now that the sun is out, much of the snow is already gone. We might have gone today were it not so muddy. I expect that the roads will be dry enough by morning."

"Excellent." There was a beat of silence between them, which was filled by the crackling of the fire. "What is the matter?"

"All is well, I assure you."

"Fitzwilliam, look at me."

Darcy obligingly turned, but not before schooling his expression into one of passive disinterest. He was a master at it.

"You are fretting again," she accused, albeit gently. *Alas, she knows me so well already.*

"Gentlemen do not *fret*," Darcy scoffed in return. "Fretting is for mothers and superstitious old women."

"Troubled, then," Elizabeth amended with fond exasperation. She moved to one end of the sofa and patted the cushion next to her. "Come and sit with me." Darcy obeyed, and she set her book aside and took up his hand. "You have done nothing of which you ought to be ashamed. All we await is a ceremony."

Elizabeth's closeness appeased some measure of Darcy's misgivings. With a sigh, he lifted her hand and pressed a kiss to the back of it. "You are right, of course, but it is in my nature to be fastidious over every small detail. I cannot help it."

"Nor would I change you for the world, but do allow me to comfort you when you ought not be so concerned. I cannot bear to see you uneasy."

"That is a fair enough compromise." He leant in and pressed his mouth softly to hers, a delicate expression of his love and one not meant to beg for anything more. When he withdrew, he lingered some seconds longer with his forehead resting against hers before changing the subject. "What are you reading?"

Elizabeth retrieved her book and opened it up to the title page. With a droll twist of her lips, she queried, "A relation of yours?"

Darcy glanced down and understood her amusement instantly. It was a novel by a Michelle D'Arcy. Laughing, he replied, "I think not. Is it any good?"

"Very. Shall I read some to you?"

They spent the remainder of the day curled up together on the sofa, taking turns reading to one another and discussing the comparative merits of prose versus poetry. Darcy was still bothered by the occasional twinge of guilt, but each was easily allayed by Elizabeth and her unrelenting cheerfulness.

CHAPTER TWENTY-THREE

"I do not like this new coachman at all," Lady Catherine groused as the carriage hit another rut in the road. "And his brother is no better. Listen to them out there, singing that bawdy nonsense. They have no notion of the deference that is due to a person of my rank."

Collins bit down hard on his own tongue. Of late, nothing he said seemed to sit well with her ladyship, and he had learnt to remain silent unless specifically asked for his opinion. Yet why should Lady Catherine not be incensed? Betrayed by her own nephew, travelling in utterly vile conditions, abandoned by her most trusted servants, and forced to spend Christmas at a dingy inn hardly fit for vermin. It was far too much to be borne by a lady of her distinction. Worst of all, the trials they endured might ultimately be for naught, due to the snowstorm that had stranded them miles from any civilised society. It was entirely possible that Mr Darcy and Cousin Elizabeth were already wed and on their return trip to Pemberley. Collins trembled at the very thought.

The carriage jerked and shuddered again. The new driver and footman were truly inadequate, but they had been the only ones available when her ladyship's former team resigned some days ago on account of the horrid weather and even worse working conditions. The louts had abandoned them at The Black Boar, a squalid establishment full of dirty glasses and unsavoury characters. Lady Catherine was fortunate enough to have secured a private room, but Collins had to spend three nights sleeping in a draughty, freezing common room amidst drunkards and ruffians. It had been an utterly miserable Christmas.

"Well, neither of them can expect any reference from *me*," Lady Catherine continued to rail. "For their own sakes, they had better not presume to ask. Disgusting, disloyal creatures."

Collins bobbed his head up and down in agreement.

Her ladyship's eyes narrowed into slits. "Have you nothing to say on this point? No apology to offer?"

"A-apology?"

"I have always considered you fairly dull, Mr Collins, but you continue to astound me with your witlessness. Must I remind you that we are on this godforsaken journey because of *your* failures?"

Though his instinct was to agree with all that her ladyship said, in this instance Collins felt her accusation was misdirected. Certainly it was his betrothed with whom Mr Darcy had run off, but that gentleman must accept his share of the blame. Had he but done his duty to his family and married Miss de Bourgh as preordained, he would never have been taken in by that grasping, wanton Elizabeth Bennet.

There must have been some mismanagement in Cousin Elizabeth's education for her to have done something so scandalous, so contrary to every notion of right, as to entice the would-be husband of another lady. Collins blamed her parents nearly as much as the hoyden herself. This licentiousness in behaviour must have proceeded from a faulty degree of indulgence.

It was—dare Collins even think it—unreasonable for Lady Catherine to heap all the blame upon him when other parties were more culpable. Of all the involved persons, he was the least at fault, in his humble opinion. But if the great lady persisted in blaming him for the profligacy of others, he might never find himself in her good graces again, and that was an intolerable prospect. His cousin Bennet was reportedly at death's door, but until the older man drew his last breath, Collins was dependent upon the charity of his patroness. Should Mr Bennet linger much longer, and should Lady Catherine's benevolence wane, Collins might be in grave trouble indeed.

Perhaps, if he was exceedingly careful how he worded his defence, she might be swayed to think better of him. "B-but am I not also a victim?"

Lady Catherine's nostrils flared. "A victim?"

"Yes! For have I not, much like your nephew, been taken

in by my cousin? She was promised to me, only to abandon me at the altar! You can be assured that I had no notion of any prior attachment to another. If I had, I would have insisted that she be watched every moment and never allowed to leave the house without someone responsible to chaperon!"

Lady Catherine's mouth was stretched into a taut line, and she observed him with burning eyes. He considered this enough encouragement to continue.

"I am as much affronted by her behaviour as your lady-ship, and once she has been made to marry me, I swear I shall keep her under better regulation. I blame her father for filling her head with false impressions of her own importance in the world. And her mother, too, for encouraging her to catch a husband by any means." He shook his head. "Cousin Elizabeth will be in much need of your advice. I shall rely upon your instruction to mould her into a proper wife, one who will not shame me further. If it were only to assuage my own feelings, I would prefer to throw her into the hedgerows with the rest of her detestable family, but as a clergyman I feel it is my duty to correct evil where I see it. She will suffer her penance and be grateful for it. Why—"

A sharp rap of her cane against his knee startled Collins into abandoning the remainder of his speech.

"Do be quiet, you insufferable simpleton! I have no inten-tion of training your disgraceful cousin into a proper lady. What can you be thinking? That I should let your wanton harlot remain at Hunsford, where my nephew can continue to meet with her? By God, you are the greatest dolt who ever lived! I have brought you with me in order to remove that chit as temptation for Darcy, but do not believe for an instant that you retain my favour still. Once I have returned to Kent, I shall petition your bishop to have you removed as my parson."

"B-but—"

"I command your silence! Frankly, I am too disgusted to look at you any longer," Lady Catherine snarled. She abruptly turned her chin to stare at the wall as she raised her cane and rapped on the roof. The carriage slowed to a trembling stop. "Get out."

"Get out?"

"Now!"

Collins peeked out of the window but saw nary a building nor a single signpost. There was no evidence of civilisation at all, nothing but bare trees, melting snow, and mud. "I cannot get out here! There might not be a village for miles. What am I to do?"

Lady Catherine's malevolent gaze remained affixed to the carriage wall, unsoftened by his plea. "That is not my concern. Leave me and do not dare to show your face in my presence again."

A shiver-inducing wind blew inside when one of the servants jerked the door open. "You be needin' sumptin', ma'am?"

"Yes, see to it that Mr Collins's trunk is unloaded. He will be walking from here."

The footman looked perturbed, but he tipped his hat and moved to do as she bade him.

Collins was becoming truly frightened. "Lady Catherine, I

know that your beneficence, your condescension, would not allow you to condemn a man to—"

"Why are you still here?"

Sensing not an ounce of sympathy in her countenance, and habitually trained to follow her every command, Collins stumbled out of the carriage onto the muddy lane. With his shoes squelching beneath him, he made one final entreaty. "Your ladyship has every right to be angry with me, but do allow me to make amends. You require someone to marry my wayward cousin. Take me with you and—"

"I shall send your shameless cousin home on the stage," Lady Catherine interrupted with vehement annoyance. "Her family may deal with her. Should you still wish to marry her, you may search for her there." Such were her final words before she signalled the driver to close the door. Despite his months of faithful service, he did not receive so much as a simple farewell.

A moment later, Collins's trunk landed next to him in a frothy slew of mud and snow, splashing him up to his waist. Frozen by the cold and his own horror, Collins watched the equipage rattle away.

———— ⚔ ————

AFTER WHAT FELT LIKE HALF A DAY LATER, BUT WHAT HIS watch insisted was only a little over two hours, Collins plodded into a village about noon. It was somewhat larger than the one in which he had spent Christmas, and the place bustled with a respectable amount of activity. However, it was missing one key element: Lady Catherine's carriage. Knowing her determination to make as few stops as possible, Collins was not surprised that she had not bothered to stop here, yet he was still disappointed. During his unplanned march through the countryside, he had composed a pretty speech which, he hoped, might assuage her ladyship's temper enough that she would welcome him back into her retinue. Alas, he could not prostrate himself if she were not present.

There was nothing for it but to go to the inn and purchase a meal and hot drink whilst he considered what to do next. He supposed he should send someone after his trunk and then secure himself a spot on the stage going south. He would not be continuing his pursuit; it was far too much trouble with no real benefit to him at this juncture. Further, he had not enough money to carry on further north, not unless he wished to starve, and would have to haggle with every coin just to get himself back home; another injury to add to his ever-lengthening letter of complaint to Mr Bennet. Collins expected reimbursement—and perhaps a bit extra—for his troubles.

The Red Hare was hardly the height of splendour and luxury, but it was far and away more respectable than The Black Boar had been. The scent of roasting meat wafted outside from the kitchens and drew Collins closer with its tantalising promise of a hearty luncheon. A pot of tea would not go amiss, either, or perhaps some strong ale. His mouth watered at the prospect, having not tasted anything worth eating in days. His purse was not as heavy as he would wish, but he could afford a meal before purchasing his ticket.

As he entered the establishment, he was inclined to be affronted by the look of distaste the proprietor gave him. Collins might be covered head to foot in muck, but he was still a clergyman and deserving of a certain amount of deference. Haughtily, he demanded, "A table. And I shall require the services of a boy to fetch my trunk from up the road."

The innkeeper raised an eyebrow. "Met with some calamity during your travels, have you?"

Collins owed this man no explanation. "Just see that it is done whilst I eat."

"'Fraid I'm going to require your payment up front…sir." The innkeeper eyed him charily.

Collins opened his mouth to administer the man a well-deserved tongue lashing. Another moment of reflection—and the sudden appearance of a pair of hulking manservants going about their business—forced him to reconsider. There were few options open to him in a village this small, and Collins did not wish to trudge however many miles it was to the next. Grumbling, he withdrew his purse and slapped a couple of coins down upon the innkeeper's desk, then another when the lout had the gall to claim one more copper was owed. It was robbery!

The innkeeper flicked his hand in the direction of the common room and wandered away, hopefully to assign a servant to retrieve the trunk. Collins sniffed and stalked to a free table to order his repast.

It was to his great surprise that midway through his mutton, he heard a familiar voice.

"...is free to attend us...I think a walk round the yard... much good."

Cousin Elizabeth? Collins searched the room for the comely figure of his runaway bride, but the only women he could see were matronly servants. Had he been mistaken?

"It is considerably cold and muddy."

No! I should know the stately cadence of Mr Darcy anywhere. Collins pushed back his chair and stepped away from the table to better survey the room at large. He rounded an oak column that blocked his view and beheld his quarry. In the vestibule, near the base of the staircase, was a couple standing indecently close together and behaving with uncommon familiarity. Although they faced away from him, the shameless hussy could be none other than Miss Elizabeth Bennet herself; Collins recognised the alluring roundness of her backside as she shifted her weight closer to the tall gentleman at her side. He, once his head tilted towards her, was confirmed to be Mr Darcy.

"True," she said, "but I shall not venture far. I only mean to stretch my legs a bit before we depart."

"Shall I escort you?"

"No, you had best stay here and complete our business. Once you are finished, we can be on our way. We are already getting a late enough start, seeing how we..."

Though her speech trailed off, her coy smile told the rest. *Wanton hussy!* Naturally his indelicate cousin would wish to walk alone in the mud; she had done so often enough since he had known her. But however much he disapproved of her uncivilised habits, she had presented him with an opportunity. It occurred to him as he watched the pair separate that this might be his only chance to redeem himself to Lady Catherine.

If I can still marry her myself and preserve Mr Darcy for Miss de Bourgh...Indeed, it was a brilliant plan. Collins waited until the gentleman was occupied with the ungracious innkeeper and stealthily slipped out after his cousin Elizabeth.

CHAPTER TWENTY-FOUR

E lizabeth wandered aimlessly, inattentive to her surroundings as she reflected on her newfound understanding of her betrothed. She and Darcy had woken that morning to discover the roads sufficiently dry for travel at last, and she contemplated how fortunate she was to be on the precipice of marrying the best of men. It was a blessing as unexpected as it was wonderful. Who could have possibly imagined that she, Elizabeth Bennet, who was always assured of her own cleverness, would so completely reverse her opinion? *Not I, certainly.* Had anyone told her in the autumn that she would fall in love with the rude, aloof Mr Darcy before the year was over, she would have been most unladylike in her response.

No matter. Everything has turned out just the way it should. I am to marry a man who loves me, and whom I love in return. Could there be any happier conclusion?

Though her sudden shift in affection for him had initially frightened her, Elizabeth could not find it in herself to repine what she was feeling. Her attachment to him had not stood the test of many months' suspense, but it was strong, and there was no prescribed amount of time for falling in love. Darcy's devotion to her happiness spoke of how truly good and selfless he was. Added to this was something yet more substantial in how he showed this devotion with uncommon respect and the ability to compromise his own inclinations for the sake of hers. *The real wonder*, she laughed to herself with some self-deprecation, *was that it took me so long to see his true qualities!*

She shook her head, dispelling any part of the past that did not bring her pleasure. They had got off on the wrong foot, it was true, but there was no point in dwelling on it when they had every reason to anticipate a joyful future together.

By tonight, I shall be Mrs Fitzwilliam Darcy. Just thinking of it created a delicious glow within Elizabeth's chest. *I shall be the best wife possible*, she promised herself, *and Fitzwilliam will have no cause to repine. Nor shall I.*

She was viciously jerked out of her happy reflections by a rough wrenching of her arm, a motion that spun her entirely round. Dazed by pain and surprise, it took Elizabeth a moment to recognise her assailant, but when she did so it was with a gasp.

"Mr Collins!"

It was, indeed, he, though looking much worse for the wear. Before he was only pungent and oily, but now he looked and smelled as if he had spent the night in a pig sty. Every part of him—his clergyman's frock, greasy hair, hostile face—was splattered with mud, dirt, and heaven knew what else. Beyond her own horror at seeing him again, Elizabeth wondered what had befallen him to bring him to this current level of dishevelment.

Mr Collins yanked her closer, bringing his nose mere inches from hers, the overpowering odour of his foul breath spilling out with his words. "I have finally caught you, you duplicitous jezebel! After so much humiliation and difficulty, I finally have you!" He then shook her so hard that her head lurched back and forth.

Though her vision was blurred and she was off-balance, Elizabeth attempted to tug her arm out of Mr Collins's grasp. "Let go! You are hurting me!"

"No more than you deserve, you ungrateful harlot." He shook her again, and she nearly fell to the muddy ground. "Let there be no mistake, you will suffer far worse before I am done with you. As your husband, it will be my duty to correct the grievous flaws in your character that have led to your outrageous misconduct. You will never shame me again!"

Elizabeth tried to pull away from him again, but Mr Collins held fast; the pressure was beginning to bruise, she could feel it. "Release me!"

"Not until we are properly man and wife. Even then, I shall be keeping a close eye on you, lest your base nature inspire you to behave so disreputably again. Come, I shall hire a cart to take us the rest of the way to Gretna Green, and we can be done with this disagreeable business once and for all."

So saying, Mr Collins began to drag her away, but Elizabeth dug the heels of her boots into the soft ground and threw her entire weight into preventing him. She would fight for her freedom with every step he forced from her. "I will never marry a brute like you! I am going to marry Mr Darcy, who will come looking for me any moment!"

At least, she hoped he would. Glancing about, Elizabeth realised that she had wandered further from the inn than she had intended. Trees bordered the lane along which she had walked, and there were no people or carriages in sight, though they could hardly be far off. Perhaps she might be heard if she screamed for aid.

Mr Collins's face was turning red with the effort of attempting to drag her up the road. "Stop this…this disgraceful behaviour and…*move!*"

Elizabeth struggled to maintain her footing, but she was losing her advantage in the slippery mud. Thrice she nearly went down, which would have left her more vulnerable than ever, but she would not give in. "Let go! I *will* wed Mr Darcy, and you cannot stop—"

Abruptly, Mr Collins ceased pulling at her and drew up close again. Elizabeth cringed as spittle flew from his lips and dotted her cheeks. "As your male relative and your superior, I demand that you cease this nonsense at once and come with me! Mr Darcy is destined for Miss de Bourgh, and you have no right to tempt him away from her. Furthermore, you are fortunate that I am still willing to have you, considering your most unbecoming conduct. However, if you do not capitulate now, I shall see you and your family thrown from Longbourn the instant your father is dead. Seeing as that shall be any day now—"

Cruelly taunted beyond endurance, Elizabeth performed the most unladylike act of her entire life: she spat in Mr Collins's eye. "You little—"

He released her to wipe away the spittle, enabling Elizabeth to stumble out of his reach. Not waiting to hear whatever invectives he conjured up next, she immediately ran back from whence she came. She was unable to best Mr Collins in strength, but she more than made up for it in swiftness, and quickly outpaced him. The inn appeared just beyond the next bend with its tell-tale arch and, yet more relief, Darcy stood in front of it. He turned to her as she approached, at first confused and then alarmed. With an inarticulate cry, she collapsed into his waiting arms.

Darcy cupped her cheeks within his palms and angled her face upwards, searching it urgently. His thumbs swiped away the tears Elizabeth had not realised she was shedding. "Good God, Elizabeth! What has happened?"

"Mr-Mr Collins…" was all Elizabeth could force out as she struggled for breath.

There was no need for further explanations, as Mr Collins plodded into the yard at that moment, wheezing insults and pointing an accusing finger at her. "Stop…stop her! She is my…my…"

Darcy released Elizabeth's face and swept her behind him, creating a formidable barrier between herself and Mr Collins. "What is the meaning of this? Chasing a young lady down the street—have you no decency?"

Mr Collins attempted to grab at Elizabeth again, but Darcy moved to block him and shoved the oaf away. The clergyman stumbled, waving his arms about in an ungainly fashion, but somehow managed to stay upright. "She...she ran from me... and...and..."

"Who would *not* run from you?" countered Darcy with so much ferocity that Collins flinched and took several steps backwards. "You are pursuing a lady like a madman! No doubt she believes you mean her violence. Unless"—Darcy glanced back at Elizabeth, his gaze searching her shivering form for signs of harm before turning back to Mr Collins—"unless you have already laid your hands upon her."

The ominous darkening of Darcy's features would have induced a more intelligent man to deny it, but Mr Collins apparently lacked the requisite sense. "She was being unreasonable. She would not come willingly! I had no choice—"

The end of Mr Collins's sentence was strangled to an abrupt halt as Darcy grabbed fistfuls of his clothing and lifted him off the ground. As the parson outweighed Darcy by several stone, this feat was all the more impressive. "I swear to God and everyone here that if you have harmed *my wife* in any way, I shall see to it that you are whipped in front of all these villagers! But not until after I have thrashed you myself."

Darcy's words prompted Elizabeth to look about her, and she saw that the courtyard and lane were filling with people.

"I was only attempting to prevent a grave wrong!" Mr Collins squealed. "Think of your actual betrothed, sir, the fair Miss de Bourgh. You have been blinded by my cousin's charms, but your duty—"

"Do not tell me of my duty," Darcy snarled. "You have no right to interfere in my affairs, whatever they may be."

Mr Collins bleated piteously and clawed at Darcy's hands, but to no avail. "But your aunt, the venerable Lady Catherine de Bourgh, expects you to marry her daughter. How can you overthrow the brightest jewel of Kent for someone so far beneath you as my cousin? With what Miss Elizabeth has done, she is no better than a…than a painted whore!"

The crowd gasped.

"I warned you before about insulting the lady's honour, Collins. Say another word against her and we meet upon the field of honour. Furthermore, whatever my aunt expects of me, it is no business of yours."

"If you will not answer to me, then you must answer to Lady Catherine! As we speak, she must already be at Gretna Green and will not allow you to take this-this…*unsuitable* girl to wife!"

Darcy yanked Mr Collins closer and whispered menacingly. "What? Lady Catherine intends to disrupt my wedding?"

"Oh yes! Your esteemed aunt will stand betwixt you and the anvil—*urk!*"

Darcy cut off Mr Collins's smug proclamation with a sharp shake that caused the man's head to snap back and forth. "You insolent worm!"

Elizabeth could not help but feel her cousin deserved this treatment after inflicting the same violence upon her. Nevertheless, hearing the whispers of those about them, she placed a hand on Darcy's shoulder and called his attention. "Mr Darcy.

Sir. *Fitzwilliam!*" The last drew his eyes to her. "Put him down and let the law deal with him."

Though Darcy's jaw remained clenched, he released Mr Collins. The pitiable clergyman crumpled to the ground in a heap, covering his head with his arms as he blubbered. A moment later, two manservants from the inn came forward and heaved him to his feet before dragging him away.

Darcy turned to Elizabeth and gently cupped her face with his hands. "Did he harm you, dearest? Should I call for an apothecary?"

Elizabeth shook her head before resting her cheek within the cradle of his palm. She was certain he could feel how severely she trembled. "I am well enough. Let us continue on," she said, then added in a lower voice, "I wish to be married as soon as possible."

Darcy nodded and inhaled a steadying breath. After barking a few orders, demanding that Mr Collins be taken directly to the local magistrate and charged with assault against a gentlewoman, he escorted Elizabeth inside. Accepting the offer of a private parlour, he closed the door, blocking out much of the uproar, and gathered her to his chest. The moment she was ensconced within his embrace, Elizabeth allowed herself to cry.

CHAPTER TWENTY-FIVE

G iving a statement to the local magistrate was necessary to see Collins locked away. Thankfully, there was little dispute over what had occurred, given Elizabeth's testimony and the number of witnesses who had observed Collins chasing her up the main street, so it was a straightforward task. Even so, it delayed them for the better part of two hours, during which time they were wild to be on their way. At last, the deed was done and Darcy was free to bundle Elizabeth into the carriage. They left Collins to the mercies of the law—and an outraged village—without a single glance backwards.

Once they were on the road again and closer than ever to their destination, Darcy allowed himself to dwell on the new obstacle ahead of them.

"My aunt has no chance of dissuading us from our course, regardless of her methods, but knowing of her trap allows us to avoid it. It should be nothing to simply sidestep her and her hollow objections. Collins was careless in revealing her machinations. It has robbed her of the element of surprise."

Elizabeth, who had clung to his side since her ordeal, lifted her head from his shoulder. "Your aunt was careless in bringing him with her."

"Knowing my aunt as I do, I suspect she brought him to impose on you in the hope that, with you married and out of my reach, I might turn my attentions upon Anne. It would not have worked, but then again, Lady Catherine often assumes others will obey her without question. Had I realised that Mr Collins would reveal our plans so soon after we left Meryton, I might have been more prepared for this outcome. Your cousin made quick work of finding her in London and rallying her to action."

Elizabeth's mouth curled into a mischievous smile. "I imagine he sought his patroness because he found no coopera-tion at Longbourn. Even were my father not"—she paused to take a shuddering breath—"so ill, I cannot believe that he would have given chase. He hates to travel and despises Mr Collins. With Jane there to attest that I had gone with you will-ingly, Papa would not have been inclined to thwart you to assist *him*."

"I would certainly hope not. One question that still plagues me, though—I cannot fathom why Lady Catherine abandoned Collins on the side of the road." The loss of his patroness's esteem was among the many charges the worthless swine had levelled against them as he defended himself before the magistrate. Darcy assumed Collins had done a thorough job of repulsing Lady Catherine himself.

"Can you not? He is not the most enjoyable of company in the best of circumstances, and I imagine she must be terribly angry with him at the moment. After all, he did nothing to prevent our elopement."

Darcy scoffed. "And how might he have accomplished that, pray tell?"

"I am sure I do not know, but from all I have heard of Lady Catherine, I suspect she is not the type of person to suffer fools or failure gladly. Mr Collins is both."

Chuckling, Darcy pressed a soft kiss to her temple. "You have her measure without even having met her. Why am I unsurprised?"

She gave him an expressive look. "I cannot say that my ability to sketch characters is flawless, but your aunt is a simple creature to understand. She enjoys having her own way, and we have not obliged her."

It was not much longer before they passed the marker denoting the Scottish border and found themselves on the outskirts of the infamous Gretna Green. Ahead, standing as a humble beacon to the impetuous couples of England, was the blacksmith's shop. In front of it was a grand carriage that Darcy would know anywhere.

He drew back from the window and closed the shade. "As we suspected, Lady Catherine is here. I propose that we drive on to the next village to avoid the unpleasantness of facing her."

Elizabeth pressed her lips together but was not entirely

successful at checking her mirth. "Are you intimidated by your aunt, sir?"

"Not at all," he asserted, though there was a modicum of truth to her teasing accusation. He and his cousins had been fearful of Lady Catherine's temper as lads, and some residual wariness remained within him still. It was, perhaps, why he had failed to decisively curtail her expectations regarding Anne years ago. She had no true power over him, but old habits were difficult to shake entirely.

With her eyes twinkling, Elizabeth conceded to his proposal. "I have no inclination to defend myself to your relatives just yet. I do not object to driving a little farther."

And so, after a few harried words to the coachman, they left Gretna Green and Darcy's disagreeable aunt behind.

⁂

HALF AN HOUR LATER, AND WITH LADY CATHERINE NONE THE wiser, Darcy and Elizabeth stood in the common room of a rustic inn. Mr Stewart, the proprietor, seemed pleased to be asked by such a wealthy gentleman to perform the ceremony, and had taken on the role with aplomb. The man gathered as many witnesses as the inn could accommodate, explaining enthusiastically that he wanted to leave no doubt the deed was done properly. Thus, though Darcy was not entirely comfortable being at the centre of a spectacle, he and Elizabeth found themselves surrounded by a large crowd of servants, guests, and curious onlookers, many of whom were attracted by the happy commotion. Darcy imagined that this hamlet, upstaged by the notorious Gretna Green, did not often see elopements.

Mr Stewart, puffing himself up to address the impromptu gathering, launched into a lengthy speech on the merits of marriage. It was somewhat difficult to discern the precise words through his thick brogue, but Darcy might have done better had he actually paid much attention to them. Instead, his full attention was on his bride, who stood before him in a silk gown the colour of candlelight. It was the same one she had worn to the Netherfield ball; he remembered it well, having spent half the evening admiring her in it. Though he had been impatient to wed immediately upon their arrival at the inn, Darcy could not begrudge her taking the time to change from her torn, muddy frock to this most elegant replacement.

Never had there been a more radiant bride. Elizabeth verily glowed in the shafts of sunlight streaming in through the windows behind her, as if touched by the divine—perhaps she was, when one recalled her fortunate escape from a different wedding. It being winter, she held no flowers, but the embroidered sprigs of white crocuses dotting the hem of her skirt made up for the lack. Her dark hair was mostly hidden beneath her bonnet, as was proper, but a few impudent tendrils had escaped and were presently dangling, glossy and inviting, against her nape. Most resplendent of all was the beaming smile she wore and the dappled light of pure joy within her eyes as she looked up. Her effervescence enthralled him.

A loud cough called Darcy's attention away from the bewitching vision and he looked to Mr Stewart. The innkeeper's face was wreathed in an indulgent smile, but his brows were raised in anticipation.

"Oh, forgive me." Darcy cleared his own throat. "I, Fitzwilliam Darcy, do declare my intention to take Miss Elizabeth Bennet as my wife."

Mr Stewart turned his gaze to Elizabeth and prompted her to respond. She, unlike her bridegroom, was prepared to answer, though she did so with apparent amusement at Darcy's expense. "I, Elizabeth Bennet, do declare my intention to take Mr Fitzwilliam Darcy as my husband."

Their troth was nearly sealed. However, Darcy had insisted on one more custom to make the occasion feel more official. With an embarrassing amount of struggle in front of so many strangers, he fished his mother's ring from his waistcoat pocket and presented it to Elizabeth on his open palm. She regarded with apparent awe the twined band of gold and diamonds, wrought together into the shape of a delicate bloom at the centre.

Darcy lifted her left hand and repeated the vows he had heard at previous weddings throughout his lifetime. Other bridegrooms had performed their roles by rote, lifelessly promising themselves to their brides as though it mattered not to them, but his voice quaked with emotion. "With this ring," he said, slipping it onto the elegant length of her finger, "I thee wed, with my body I thee worship, and with all my worldly goods I thee endow. In the name of the Father, and of the Son, and of the Holy Ghost. Amen."

Elizabeth stared at their conjoined hands, her lashes flickering rapidly as if staving off tears, and she flushed with some strong emotion. When she looked up at him, he knew instantly what it was: love. Overflowing, unadulterated, and unqualified love. *How I long to kiss her.*

His desire must have been obvious to everyone in the room, for no sooner had Mr Stewart drawn the short ceremony to a close than the crowd began cheering for Darcy to give his bride a *smooriken*. He reddened at their entreaties to perform such an intimate act in public, but was not unwilling. He searched Elizabeth's face to gauge her feelings. When she responded to his wordless question with a blushing nod, his hesitation was forgot. He cupped her cheeks with his hands, lowered his head, and pressed his lips to hers as applause and huzzahs erupted about them.

CHAPTER TWENTY-SIX

Elizabeth's knees shook like jelly as her new husband escorted her up the front stairs of Pemberley with far more ceremony than their rustic Scottish wedding had called for. Never in her wildest dreams had she imagined that she, simple Elizabeth Bennet from a market town in Hertfordshire, would warrant so much fuss on the occasion of her marriage. *But then, I am no longer Elizabeth Bennet, am I?*

On either side of them was a veritable battalion of servants, gathered in straight lines to greet their new mistress as though she were a queen. She was, in a way, now that she was the wife of so august a personage as Fitzwilliam Darcy, nephew of an earl and one of the wealthiest landowners across all of England. Only rarely had she appreciated just how very grand Darcy was, and never had this grandeur so overpowered her senses. She only hoped that she might live up to the expectations.

More daunting than the orderly queue of servants, however, were the people who awaited them at the top of the mansion's stairs. Darcy's sister stood demurely before the impressive set of double doors, flanked by a matronly housekeeper and an austere butler. The three of them together presented an imposing image to the new bride.

Elizabeth swallowed and bolstered her courage, refusing to be intimidated by her own misplaced sense of inferiority. Pemberley might well be the most magnificent manor she had ever seen, the servants more dignified than most of her acquaintance, and the lineage of her new sister impeccable, but she was one of them now. *I am Elizabeth Darcy. I shall rise to the challenge.*

Up close, Miss Darcy was far less intimidating than Elizabeth had supposed from afar. The young lady was tall, built on a larger scale than herself and with the figure of a woman, but the way she bounced on her toes and rushed forward to greet them revealed her true age. She was better behaved than Kitty and Lydia, to be sure, but her bubbling enthusiasm was familiar to all adolescent girls.

"Brother, welcome home!"

Elizabeth smiled at how Miss Darcy glanced between her and Darcy with eagerness and an endearing touch of bashfulness, clearly wishing to be more bold. She seemed unable to decide how to act, echoing Elizabeth's own feelings.

Darcy, apparently not beset by any of the nerves that plagued his new wife or dear sister, presented Elizabeth with pride. "Georgiana, I would like you to meet my wife, Elizabeth. Elizabeth, this is my sister, Georgiana Darcy."

The ladies curtseyed to one another before Darcy placed his hand at the small of Elizabeth's back to direct her towards the senior servants, both of whom were waiting patiently to be acknowledged.

"This is Mr Bartholomew, Pemberley's butler, and our housekeeper, Mrs Reynolds."

Mr Bartholomew gave a deep bow, while Mrs Reynolds folded into a low curtsey, which was most impressive for her apparent age. As with Miss Darcy, the housekeeper was not so frightening up close; her eyes crinkled with an earnest kindness that promised a certain amount of indulgence for her master's new wife. Elizabeth felt instinctively that whatever her failings as mistress, Mrs Reynolds could be relied upon to guide and correct her with forbearance. This realisation, while it did not assuage all of Elizabeth's self-doubt, put her more at ease in her new surroundings.

"Shall we adjourn to the green parlour?" Miss Darcy suggested. "I have ordered some refreshments in anticipation of your arrival."

The couple agreed with alacrity, and they stepped across the threshold as one.

"I was so excited to receive your last," Miss Darcy exclaimed once the servants had withdrawn and the tea was poured. "You may confirm it with Mrs Reynolds, I was beside myself when you declared you were to be home in only two days! I hardly knew what to do first, have your chambers aired out or plan tonight's dinner."

Darcy seemed pleasantly astonished. "Indeed? I see Mrs Annesley's influence has been a good one if you have done so much to prepare for our arrival."

"Oh yes, I could not have done it without her. She helped Mrs Reynolds redirect my energies after that first burst of excitement."

"And where is your companion?"

"Lying down. She went to bed with a fever last evening, but she seems to be somewhat better today." Swiftly returning to the previous subject with cheerful impatience, Miss Darcy said, "I have greatly anticipated your homecoming since you departed London, and have been most eager to meet my new sister." Miss Darcy glanced shyly at Elizabeth before withdrawing her eyes back to Darcy.

"As I have been eager to meet you," Elizabeth was rewarded with a bright smile. "Mr Darcy has told me much of you on our journey. Many little secrets privy to an older brother," she added with a wink.

Miss Darcy looked to her brother with alarm. "He-he has?"

Elizabeth felt contrition tingling in her cheeks at her unintentional reference to Miss Darcy's folly from the previous summer. Hastily, she sought to reassure the girl. "Indeed, I feel like I know you already. I know you prefer Haydn to Mozart, have a real talent for capturing a scene with watercolours, and detest sewing nearly as much as I do. Your brother's information does not go so far as to inform me if you prefer reading to cards, but then we must discover some of these things ourselves."

Darcy, who had frozen momentarily as the discomfort between his wife and sister permeated the room, gave Elizabeth an approving nod over his teacup and took a leisurely sip. The awkward moment had passed without need for his intervention, and she felt relieved that he seemed content to let them carry on the conversation without him for the nonce.

And so they did for several minutes until Miss Bingley was unexpectedly mentioned. Miss Darcy—or Georgiana, as she insisted on being called, now that they were sisters—was describing the tumult at Darcy House in the wake of Darcy's sudden departure. "And Miss Bingley turned greener than her gown when she saw for herself you were not there!"

"Miss Bingley?" Darcy repeated, his mouth puckering as if he had tasted something sour.

Elizabeth and Georgiana exchanged glances full of shared mirth before the latter replied, "Yes, indeed. Did I not tell you that Miss Bingley came looking for you the morning you left? She pretended she was there to see me, of course, but I am hardly such a simpleton as to believe that. I cannot fathom how she knew where you went, but when I confirmed it she looked notably ill."

"I assume Bingley left her some sort of note. He came with me to Hertfordshire."

At Georgiana's curious look, Elizabeth explained, "Mr Bingley fell in love with my dear sister Jane whilst he stayed in Hertfordshire over the autumn. Unless I am wholly mistaken in their regard for one another, I suspect that they are now engaged."

Elizabeth watched for any sign of disappointment in Georgiana's features but saw only dawning clarity. Despite not knowing her new sister well as of yet, the girl had impressed her as one ill adept at disguising her feelings with any great success. Whatever Miss Bingley had penned in her note to Jane back in November, it seemed that Georgiana had no expectations of her brother's friend.

"Poor Miss Bingley," Georgiana said without any real sympathy. "To be so thwarted in her schemes to connect herself to our family."

Darcy scoffed loudly, then blushed when the ladies turned to him. "Forgive me. That slipped out."

Struggling not to reveal her amusement at her husband's expense, Elizabeth said to Georgiana, "I think Miss Bingley should consider herself satisfied, in the end. It may not have occurred in the way she hoped for, but she will be related to the Darcys by marriage through my sister."

Darcy rolled his eyes, and Elizabeth bit her lip in a bid not to laugh aloud at his petulance.

"That is true," Georgiana said, nodding thoughtfully. "Oh, I nearly forgot! Miss Bingley was not my only visitor. The next day, as I was readying myself for the journey to Pemberley, Lady Matlock and Cousin Richard called."

Darcy regarded his sister warily. "I hope you were not discomposed by their visit."

"Perhaps at first, but when I realised they were not there to scold me or rail against you, I was much relieved. They charged me to inform you, assuming I would see you before they did, that you are not to make any statements regarding your wedding until you have spoken to Lord Matlock."

Darcy remained stiff with suspicion. "Did they say why?"

"Well, my aunt would not be specific with me, but Richard told me secretly that they hope to hush up your elopement and disguise it as a private family affair instead. They were on their way to Oak Grove Manor with the purpose of making it seem as though they were travelling to see you married. Lord Matlock wishes you to write to him immediately to let him know that you have arrived."

"And did Richard mention how they expected to handle Lady Catherine?" Darcy's brow was raised in challenge.

Georgiana lifted one dainty shoulder in a shrug. "Only that with the rest of the family conspiring to hush up the scandal, she would hardly be believed. Or such is their hope."

Elizabeth doubted Lady Catherine's accusations of infamous conduct would be so easily swept away, but supposed there was nothing else to be done for it. She and Darcy were already married, and seemed to have the grudging support of most of his nearest relations. There would always be those amongst the *ton* who would disparage their union for one reason or another. Any hateful whispers of the truth of their hasty nuptials might affect Georgiana when she came out in two or three years, but hopefully this would be mitigated by the tacit approval of the earl and his family. Only time would tell for sure.

"I shall write to my uncle once we have settled in. We may as well invite them to Pemberley to begin whatever farce they deem necessary," Darcy declared with obvious impatience and perhaps a touch of relief. "In the meantime, I am tired from our journey. Let us adjourn to our chambers for now and meet again for dinner."

The ladies agreed and, with the promise between Elizabeth and Georgiana to sing duets later that evening, they parted.

***

UPSTAIRS, ELIZABETH AGAIN EXPERIENCED THE SAME SENSE OF awe she had felt upon arriving at Pemberley earlier that afternoon. The mistress's rooms had been aired and thoroughly cleaned, no doubt thanks to the attentions of Georgiana, Mrs Reynolds, and goodness knows how many chambermaids and footmen.

The apartment was spacious and richly appointed with thick rugs, luxurious draperies, and opulent upholstery, all in shades of the most delicate pink and shimmering gold. It was more ornate than Elizabeth would have chosen for herself, but Lady Anne had good taste; the rooms were well-planned and handsome, not gaudy or uselessly fine. Each piece of furniture had been chosen for its utility as well as its beauty, Elizabeth thought as she trailed her fingers idly across the surface of a writing desk and admired its details. She could envision herself sitting here every morning to tend her correspondence in the warm light cascading in from the nearby window— provided that she was not too distracted by the bucolic view of Pemberley's grounds.

And what a view it is! Though Elizabeth would always hold a fondness for the gently rolling hills of her home county, she had to admit that the grandeur of the peaks suited her very well, indeed. Much like her new home, the rocks and mountains rose naturally from their surroundings, benevolently overseeing all that lay within their purview. Elizabeth would never tire of gazing at them in the near distance, feeling insignificant in the shadow of their might.

There was a tightening in her chest that heralded the return of the sense of inadequacy Elizabeth had banished at the manor's threshold. *Of all this I am mistress*, she thought with rising dismay. *Of all this I am responsible, yet I know not how to care for it. How long will it take for Fitzwilliam's disappointment to become apparent? He, who was born to steward these lands, cannot forever hide his disdain for my ineptitude and ignorance. What shall I do when his admiration fades?*

The slight creak of a door hinge rang loudly in Elizabeth's ears, and she knew that her husband approached. She inhaled deeply, intent upon hiding her distress, and turned to him with a bright smile she did not feel. "Fitzwilliam, there you are! I had hoped you would not abandon me to find my way back down to the parlour by myself. I shall require at least two weeks of familiarity with my new home, and perhaps a detailed map, before I can accomplish such a journey on my own."

Darcy halted several feet away from her, his eyes narrowed in minute observation. "Are you well, dearest?"

"Of course!" Elizabeth proclaimed, though her eyes darted away from him as she spoke. "I have been admiring the view. It is spectacular."

"Elizabeth."

Glancing up, Elizabeth discovered by the expression on his face that her false cheer had not deceived him for an instant. She sighed as her shoulders slumped. "I am merely over-whelmed, that is all. I had not expected Pemberley to be so... so...*vast* when I agreed to run away with you. Ridiculous, I know, but I do not believe it occurred to me how important you were until we arrived here and I saw all this." Elizabeth waved her hand vaguely at the room and towards the window at her back. "It is all terribly daunting, and I worry that I shall disappoint you."

Darcy closed the remaining space between them, took Elizabeth by the hands, and fixed her with an earnest look that spoke of his deep devotion. "You can never disappoint me, my love. Have you forgot? I am a gentleman, you are a gentle-man's daughter; we are equal."

Elizabeth snorted and looked down at her shoes, which peeked out from beneath the hem of her simple gown. "In station, perhaps, but not in consequence. I have not been raised with so much splendour, and that fact cannot be hidden forever. When it becomes apparent, I worry that you will find cause to regret your hasty choice." She blinked rapidly, but the tears would not be kept entirely at bay.

Darcy's hand rose to cup her cheek and wipe the anguish away. "Elizabeth, look at me." When she did not, he repeated, "Look at me." She relented at last, and he continued, "I will never grow tired of you. I will never regret marrying you. I might not look back upon our earliest days with complete satisfaction—largely due to my own unpardonable behaviour—but there is no doubt in my mind that making you my wife was the wisest thing I have ever done. I would only have repined if I had allowed you to marry Mr Collins."

Moisture continued to stream down Elizabeth's face, the torrent all the more powerful for her relief in hearing Darcy's declarations of enduring regard and adoration. Choking back waves of emotion, she managed to say in response, "I love you. I shall always love you."

He then kissed her, and the distress that had so oppressed her melted away in a haze of bliss. They sent their regrets to Georgiana for missing dinner, preferring one more evening of privacy before they must face the rest of the world together.

CHAPTER TWENTY-SEVEN

Dearest Papa,

I hope this letter finds you better than I fear. I confess, the state of your health haunts me hourly, considering what it was when I last saw you. I am wretched with guilt that my actions might have caused you any sort of harm. Do write back so that I might know how you fare and whether I can do anything for your comfort.

Oh, Papa, I beg that you would forgive me for all of my trespasses against you and my family. Jane insisted that you would understand, perhaps even approve, under the circumstances, but what I have done is selfish, and I cannot help feeling the utmost remorse for putting you, Mama, and my sisters in this situation. I apologise most sincerely for risking your health and our respectability as a family, and I hope you can find it in your heart to absolve me for my impetuousness.

Though I am deeply sorry for the way I behaved, you may take comfort that I am very happy with Mr Darcy. He is everything Mr Collins is not—intelligent, well read, honourable, loyal, kind, honest, and loving. He is also rich and handsome, which I know you would tease me are at least as important as the rest. I might not have liked him when we first knew him, but I love him now so dearly that I cannot imagine binding myself to any other. I believe you will like him almost as well when you have the opportunity to truly know him. Do say that you will allow us that opportunity and let us visit Longbourn.

You ought not to expect Mr Collins to return there with any quickness. When last I heard of him, he was in gaol, arrested for assault and attempting to abduct me. Rest assured that I am uninjured and that Mr Darcy defended me heroically.

My wedding announcement will appear in the London newspapers by the end of the week. I am certain Mama will wish to see it and show it to her friends. But on that note, I would ask a favour of you. Mr Darcy's relations have insisted that we keep the true nature of our wedding secret and say that it was merely a private ceremony attended by only close kin. I must say that I agree with them; just think of the repercussions for my sisters should the truth be widely known. To that end, I ask that you counsel Mama and the younger girls to say only that Mr Darcy came to ask for my hand and insisted upon an early date for the nuptials, wishing to bring me home to Pemberley before winter set in. Do be firm with them in adhering to the accepted story.

I shall close by reiterating my apologies for placing you all in this most irregular situation, and praying that Mr Darcy and I shall have the privilege of being received soon at Longbourn.

Your humble and repentant daughter,

Elizabeth Darcy

Elizabeth sighed and set her pen aside, still unhappy with the latest draft of her missive. She had been crafting it since yesterday but, maddeningly, was still unsure what was amiss. "It should not be so difficult to write to my own father!" she muttered to herself.

"Are you still working on that letter?"

She jumped at her husband's voice and turned in her chair to face him. "You startled me!"

Darcy stood in the open doorway between their chambers, regarding her with concern. "My sincerest apologies, dearest. Are you still struggling with writing to your father?"

Elizabeth heaved another sigh and turned back to her writing desk. She rubbed at her tired eyes and frowned at the many crossings and blotches. "Yes. I am not sure what else I can do to improve it."

A warm hand descended upon her shoulder. "May I?"

She nodded her permission and Darcy picked up the letter, careful to handle it by the edges where there were fewer splotches. He read it quickly and silently before setting it down again.

"I see nothing amiss here. Aside from writing out a clean copy, I should say it is an excellent letter."

"I feel…anxious about it. There is something wrong in its composition, or…or…I am not sure." Elizabeth slumped back against Darcy, revelling in his comforting warmth and the soothing, familiar scent of his shaving soap.

"If I were to conjecture," he said gently, "I would say that there is naught wrong with the letter itself, but rather the letter writer."

"What do you mean?"

"I believe you are still fearful of your father's reaction to our elopement, but you should not be. He loves you, Elizabeth, and he will forgive you. He likely has already."

Biting her lip, she asked in a meek voice, "Do you truly believe that?"

Darcy leant down and kissed her softly. Against her lips, he whispered, "I do." After straightening again, he continued, "Send your letter. If you have not heard back from him with a reply full of reconciliation within a fortnight, I shall be very much surprised."

Upon her dear husband's advice, Elizabeth wrote out a fair copy and sent it, along with other missives to her mother and sisters, with that day's post. She was not entirely satisfied with her efforts but prayed they would suffice.

DARCY PROVED CORRECT IN HIS BELIEF THAT MR BENNET'S forgiveness would be swift and complete. Scarcely more than a week after Elizabeth's letters were dispatched, he burst into her sitting room, waving a stack of post above his head. "You have word from Longbourn."

Elizabeth, who had been attempting to conquer the household budget, looked up from her ledger with a jolt. "So quickly?"

"Indeed."

There were six letters in all, one from each member of her immediate family. Her mother's, in particular, appeared to be bursting with words; whether they were ones of praise or reproach was yet to be seen. Her breathing quickened as she beheld the familiar, masculine handwriting of her father. What sort of response should she expect from *that* quarter?

"Come."

Elizabeth glanced up to find Darcy's hand extended to her. She placed her own within his and allowed him to lead them both to the chaise before the fireplace. This simple manoeuvre did much to settle her nervous flutterings.

"Whatever that letter says," said Darcy, his hand resting reassuringly upon her knee, "I am here."

Elizabeth swallowed, nodded, and released the seal with trembling fingers.

My precious Lizzy,

I shall begin by assuring you of my good health. I am no longer a young man, but since your flight to Gretna Green, my vigour has greatly improved, and I am not the veritable wraith you left behind. Mr Jones says it is remarkable and, should I continue so, I might live for another year or two yet. Let us all hope that proves to be the case.

On the subject of absolution, I cannot forgive you because there is nothing to forgive. Indeed, it is not I who is most deserving of an apology, but you. I am sorry, my Lizzy, that you were ever burdened by my inaction and irresponsibility. I know you will say the situation demanded that I insist upon your marrying Mr Collins, who is apparently a brute on top of being merely stupid, but I cannot absolve myself so easily. Had I done my duty and laid by an annual sum for the better provision of my family, instead of spending my whole income, I might have been able to stand by your initial rejection of his suit.

I bear you no ill-will for absconding with your Mr Darcy, considering the life you would have endured had you married my idiot cousin. Far from objecting to your elopement, I applaud your daring—you have resolved everything in such a fortuitous manner which I could never have imagined. Of course, your Mr Darcy is to be lauded as well, for his mettle and determination in bringing about this happy conclusion. It will be no hardship to call such an estimable gentleman son.

I have spoken sternly to your mother and sisters on the importance of keeping to the sanctioned version of events. Jane and Mr Bingley have been enlisted to assist me in ensuring their discretion and compliance. In short, my dear, I will not disappoint you again.

I not only allow you the dubious pleasure of visiting

Longbourn, but insist upon it. Jane will undoubtedly inform you of the particulars in her letter, but I hope you will come for a certain felicitous occasion in February, if not before. I shall say no more, as I am certain your sister wishes to do her own honours on that score. My door is, as it has always been, open to you—and now to your husband as well, if he proves to be as well read as you say.

Your loving Papa,

T Bennet

As Elizabeth finished her father's letter, she felt a handkerchief pressed into her hand. She thanked her sweet husband and dabbed it against her eyelashes to absorb the tears that had formed there. "I am so relieved!"

Darcy tucked her against his side and pressed a soft kiss to the top of her head. "I am glad. It seems that all's well that ends well, as the bard says."

"It seems so."

In the same packet of letters was another from Jane with the promised news of a most joyous event. She opened this one with far less trepidation and eagerly read it aloud.

Dearest Lizzy,

I was so relieved to receive your letter and hear that you are well and happily married. Mr Bingley has assured me time and again that his friend is an honourable man, but we knew him so little during our short acquaintance and I feared that you might not like him any better for knowing him more intimately. I am glad my worries were baseless!

Do tell me all about Mr Darcy by return post, as I should like to know more of my new brother.

I shall soon be able to tell you more of your new brother, for I am engaged to Mr Bingley! We are to marry on February 14, and I daresay I am the happiest woman in the world. The only dark cloud is that my future sisters will not be present due to Caroline's recent state of ill-health. My dear Charles informs me that she has developed a nervous condition of some sort, similar to what our mother suffers, and requires the constant attendance of a London physician. Louisa, of course, will host her in town and aid in her recovery. As disappointed as I am, I hope that you, at least, will indulge me and say you will come. I will also be so bold as to request that you and Mr Darcy spend some weeks in Hertfordshire, for you are greatly missed at Longbourn.

Lady Matlock sounds like a most kind and gracious woman. From what you have detailed in your last, the ball she is planning on your behalf will be a splendid event, and Mr Bingley and I should be most pleased to accept your invitation. I can hardly believe that I shall be a married woman by then! I feel that you have decided rightly to exclude our youngest sisters, given their occasional unruly behaviour in company, but I do beg you to extend one to my future sisters; I know they would be wild to attend a ball hosted by a countess, and I am certain Caroline's health will be much improved by then.

Your loving sister,

Jane Bennet

"Might we go, Fitzwilliam? I should dearly love to see Jane married." Elizabeth turned to present her husband with wide, pleading eyes.

Darcy chuckled at her. "You need not use such under-handed tactics, my love. I can deny you nothing, as you are well aware. We shall need to leave a little earlier for town than anticipated, but that is easily arranged."

She rewarded him with a soft kiss, which turned fervent in a moment. Fortunately, it was a meagre distance from the sitting room to the bedchamber.

———— ✠ ————

DARCY WAS NOT SO FORTUNATE IN HIS CORRESPONDENCE AS Elizabeth. Several weeks after his return to Pemberley, a letter arrived from Lady Catherine that left no one in question of her opinion of them or the subject of their marriage.

Darcy,

I am disgusted with you. What do I find upon returning to Rosings? An impudent letter boasting of your dishon-ourable conduct with the low-born bride of another man. If it were not reprehensible enough that you have overthrown Anne for this country nobody, you also have the audacity to send such a letter? Obstinate, headstrong boy, I am ashamed of you! Your mother, had she lived, would have been sickened by your behaviour. The shades of Pemberley are now polluted not only by your so-called 'wife'—whom I shall never address as Mrs Darcy, for it is not her right— but also your own infamy. I am most seriously displeased!

Exiled from Pemberley? Ha! I have no wish to see my sister's former home in the hands of Miss Bennet, to witness with my own eyes Anne's place usurped by that chit. If anyone is to be excluded, it is yourselves; taking into account your betrayal and further disrespect, you and that girl should consider yourselves banned forthwith from Rosings Park, effective immediately. I shall not participate in this farce of a marriage—I refuse!

I have been persuaded by my brother, against my inclinations, to at least keep my disgust of you and Miss Bennet within the family. Do not think for a moment that I maintain my silence for you! To the contrary, I would love nothing more than to expose your marriage for what it is, a sordid display of witless lust and avarice. No, I keep my peace for the sake of my daughter, who is innocent in these proceedings. May you long suffer the guilt belonging to you for leaving her heart-broken. Shame on you!!!

Lady Catherine de Bourgh

Upon being read once through, this piece of vitriol was thrown directly into the fire and entirely forgot.

ONE PARTICULAR LETTER CAME AS A SURPRISE TO ELIZABETH. It was addressed in a vaguely familiar hand, though she could not place the sender until she opened it and read its contents.

My dear Mrs Darcy,

How pleased I was to hear of your nuptials! I do wish I could have been there myself. Do tell me all the details— who was there? What colour was your gown? I long to know everything!

By the by, a pretty little bird has mentioned that there is to be a ball in your honour hosted by the Countess of Matlock this coming Season. Though I shall sadly not be present for my brother's wedding in February, I should dearly love to attend your soirée and convey to you my congratulations in person, should you feel inclined to extend an invitation. I know my sister, Louisa, would also adore the opportunity to communicate her well wishes to you and Mr Darcy.

Regardless, I look forward to seeing you in town very soon. We must arrange a shopping trip together; I know all of the best establishments and would be pleased to intro- duce you at court. Do encourage Lady Matlock and dear Georgiana to accompany us—what a merry party we shall make!

Ever yours,

Caroline Bingley

As it happened that Elizabeth would much rather not endure Miss Bingley's fawning attentions more than absolutely necessary, she endeavoured in her answer to put an end to any grasping pretensions. Some incentive to keep her peace would be required, but in no way would Elizabeth offer a steady friendship.

Miss Bingley,

I thank you for your kind wishes on the event of my marriage. It was a small affair, as you know, and attended by only a select few; no one of your acquaintance besides myself and Mr Darcy, I am afraid. You likely would have recognised my gown, as it was the same one I wore to the Netherfield ball, and I recall your making some comment on the sleeves when last we saw one another. I might have had one made up new, but as you know, my wedding was somewhat precipitous, and there was no time. It was a lovely occasion, however, and I have no cause to repine my choice of either gown or husband.

On the subject of Lady Matlock's ball, I shall happily add you, as well as Mr and Mrs Hurst, to the guest list so long as you do not feel such a grand event will aggravate your nervous condition. On that score, my mother has often lauded the efficacy of smelling salts whenever a spell should come upon her, and I advise you to consider keeping them close at hand. Unfortunately, I doubt that a shopping trip can be arranged beforehand, as I shall be much occupied in assisting my new aunt in all those little arrangements which must necessarily go into preparing for a ball, but perhaps we shall cross paths on Bond Street.

Yours &c,

Elizabeth Darcy

After rereading her missive to reassure herself that her message had been polite while her disinclination for Miss Bingley's company was unmistakable, Elizabeth set it on the salver to go out with the rest of the post.

CHAPTER TWENTY-EIGHT

"Lady Michelle, welcome to Pemberley." Elizabeth curtseyed and urged her guest to be seated. Since coming to Pemberley a month prior, she had been accepting callers in the green sitting room, it being the most impressive available. The neighbourhood here was more exalted than in her native Hertfordshire and, as a new bride, it was important to make a good impression. Or so encouraged Lady Matlock, who was a frequent visitor herself and a regular source of advice, most of which was unsolicited but kindly given. Elizabeth was glad to have her new aunt by her side during many of these calls.

Lady Michelle Browning appeared to be one of the friendlier denizens of Derbyshire, for she offered Elizabeth a pleasant smile as she settled herself upon a chair. She was older than her hostess by a handful of years, likely close to

Mrs Gardiner's age, and dressed in appropriately elegant attire. Some of the other ladies of the neighbourhood had bedecked themselves in an absurd amount of feathers and lace for their introduction to the new Mrs Darcy, but Lady Michelle apparently felt no need for such posturing.

Lady Matlock, who had come to Pemberley that day with the purpose of making plans for the Season, offered Lady Michelle her own welcome. "It is delightful to see you again. I have not had the pleasure of your company since we last met in town."

"At Lady Metcalf's soirée—yes, I remember. A lovely evening, if a bit of a crush."

After this exchange of pleasantries, Lady Michelle turned back to Elizabeth. "I am pleased to make your acquaintance, Mrs Darcy. I have not been to Pemberley in some time, but my husband, Sir David, considers Mr Darcy a good friend. I hope we shall become so as well."

Elizabeth answered with a smile of her own. "That would be lovely. When we return to Pemberley in the summer, I hope you will join us for a house party so we might become better acquainted."

Lady Michelle nodded with pleasure. "We would be delighted, of course. You are going to town for the Season, I take it?"

"Actually, my sister Jane is to be married on the fourteenth, so we are soon for Hertfordshire. After that, yes, we shall remain in London for a time. Lady Matlock is planning a ball in April to celebrate our marriage."

"Indeed," said Lady Matlock with a fond look for Elizabeth. "Lord Matlock and I agreed that we ought to properly welcome our new niece to the family, especially given the small, private nature of their wedding. We would be delighted if your ladyship could come to the ball."

Elizabeth found herself once again grateful that not all of Darcy's relations were as belligerent as Lady Catherine. Truthfully, she liked the countess and her family a great deal; Lady Matlock was a gracious, reasonable woman, and her husband was of the same mould. They were reserved and suspicious at first, as one might expect, but it had not taken many days before their disapprobation melted away in the face of their nephew's incontrovertible felicity. Darcy's affection for Elizabeth was obvious, as was hers for him. Their elder son was a bit pompous, but Elizabeth detected no malice in Lord Marbury, while the colonel was full of cheerful bonhomie and amusing childhood tales of Darcy. So far, they all got on quite well, considering the circumstances. She had yet to meet Lady Smithfield but would do so at the ball.

"How wonderful! I am certain it will be a splendid occasion." Lady Michelle turned to Elizabeth. "And do accept my heartfelt congratulations to your family, and your sister in particular. Your mother must be so pleased to marry off two daughters in such quick succession."

A wry smile tugged at the corners of Elizabeth's lips as she recalled her mother's last letter. Mrs Bennet was entirely beside herself to be the mother of the new Mrs Darcy; two full pages, crossed, had not been enough to express her delight at

Elizabeth marrying a man of such worth. "Indeed she is. Mr Bingley is an excellent gentleman, and I am sure he and my sister will be very happy together. As an added benefit, they will be settling only three miles from my childhood home."

"How wonderful."

It *was* wonderful. In her frequent letters, Jane expressed how happy she was to remain so near her beloved family after her marriage. Elizabeth might have felt a twinge of envy to be so far away in Derbyshire had her apprehension of facing her father in the wake of her clandestine elopement not dampened it. Mr Bennet said in his letters that he anticipated her return with much joy, but Elizabeth would not be entirely easy until she spoke to him directly and she could discern the sincerity in the lines of his face and the tone of his voice. She also longed to see this greatly improved vigour he and Jane boasted of.

"You have said your wedding was a small one, with only family present?" Lady Michelle commented.

Elizabeth lowered her cup into its saucer with a gentle rattle, the much practised story at the tip of her tongue. "Yes, it was a small ceremony. Mr Darcy wished to bring me back to Pemberley before the new year, and that did not allow much time for a large celebration."

"Young men are so impatient nowadays. I learnt of Mrs Darcy's existence in the same letter I was invited to her wedding!" Lady Matlock dissembled with practised ease. "But then again, my nephew has always known what he wants and immediately goes after it. His choice in this instance did not suffer from his impetuousness, thankfully."

"It certainly did not!" concurred Lady Michelle. "I cannot fault Mr Darcy's impatience. Travel is gruelling in the winter, and he was right to want to be at home before the frightful weather rendered the roads impassable. But why did you not plan for an autumn ceremony?"

Elizabeth bit her lip to suppress yet another smile; Lady Michelle had an uncanny talent for skirting close to the truth, yet remaining entirely ignorant of it. "We have only been acquainted since October."

"October?"

"Hence the reason we were all so behindhand when Darcy announced he was getting married!" Lady Matlock interjected with a teasing look directed at her niece.

"I can imagine. However, I have heard it said—a scandalous falsehood, I am sure—that Mr Darcy was engaged elsewhere. To his cousin, Miss de Bourgh, in fact." Lady Michelle's aspect remained placid, but she glanced between the other ladies with palpable interest.

Lady Matlock waved her hand with a nonchalant air. "Who knows how these rumours get started. I can say with certainty that there was never anything to it. In truth, Miss de Bourgh's health prevented her from marrying anyone until recently. She is much improved now, thank heaven, and prepared to partake of the upcoming Season in hopes of making a suitable match. There are a few interested parties already."

Elizabeth hid a smirk, knowing that Colonel Fitzwilliam thought his chances were fair, now that his wealthier cousin had taken himself out of contention. She had wished him luck garnering Lady Catherine's approval; Darcy had abstained with a roll of his eyes.

Lady Michelle regarded Elizabeth with a knowing press of her lips. "But in your case, it was love at first sight, I take it?"

Though tempted to chuckle, Elizabeth had become a great proficient in reining in her impish responses to this question. "Something like that."

"Sadly, I did not express myself well at our first meeting, and so my dear wife did not share my initial infatuation. Fortunately, her temper is not so resentful as my own, and she forgave my initial misstep."

The ladies turned to the entry, where Darcy stood in the doorway. His lips were lifted wryly in his wife's direction, an expression she mirrored back at him. "Once I understood him better, I found that Mr Darcy greatly improves on further acquaintance," Elizabeth said.

There was a long, heated stretch of silence between the married couple before Lady Matlock delicately cleared her throat to remind them that they were not alone. "What do you do here, Nephew?" she enquired. "I thought my sons had dragged you off to the billiard room for the afternoon."

Darcy crossed the room, kissed his aunt on the cheek, and shrugged. "I escaped."

As he sat next to Elizabeth on the sofa, Lady Michelle said, "Mr Darcy, how delighted I am to see you again. My husband sends his warmest regards."

"When we return to Derbyshire after the Season, I shall invite him to come shooting."

"Yes, your dear wife just informed me that you are for

Hertfordshire soon, and then to town. I do hope your journey will be an easy one."

Darcy's smile broadened slightly as he glanced at Elizabeth. "As do I."

———— ⚬✕⚬ ————

WHEN THE PROPER QUARTER OF AN HOUR FOR A VISIT HAD elapsed, Lady Michelle bid the Darcys a polite farewell and left. Lady Matlock, claiming fatigue with a knowing twinkle in her eye, dismissed herself to rest, leaving the couple blessedly alone.

"How did you like Lady Michelle?" Darcy asked Elizabeth as he led her back to the sofa. He hoped that her ladyship might prove to be a friend to his new wife, as she had always struck him as a kind, practical woman not prone to flights of arrogance. Additionally, he greatly liked her husband; the pair of them together would make excellent companions.

"I liked her very well indeed," replied Elizabeth. "She seems amiable and wears only the appropriate amount of lace. I believe we could be friends, if allowed the chance."

"I agree. I believe you two have much in common."

Elizabeth nodded and then lapsed into silence, her gaze vacant on the fire blazing in the hearth across from them. Darcy, recognising the import of that distant stare, squeezed her hand and recalled her attention to himself. "All will be well, my dearest. I cannot imagine that you have anything to fear from our Hertfordshire visit."

Sighing, Elizabeth laid her head against his shoulder. "I know you are right, of course, but I cannot help being a touch nervous. Do not tell my father or he will tease me mercilessly!"

Darcy chuckled and pressed a soft kiss to the crown of his dear wife's head. "I shall guard your secret but remind you again that your worries are baseless. Your family is eagerly anticipating seeing you again, and I am certain that your reunion will be a happy one. You must not fret so."

"If I recall correctly, fretting is only for mothers and superstitious old women, and I am neither."

"All the more reason for you to cease immediately."

Elizabeth swatted at Darcy's chest, and he unleashed a snuffled laugh into her hair.

"I know in my mind that my concerns are baseless, but I *have* betrayed their trust."

"Nonsense," Darcy countered. "You acted with much bravery and enriched the lives of everyone who knows you, mine especially. One could argue that your removing the problem of Mr Collins from Longbourn has extended your father's life, thus ensuring that your mother and sisters will keep their home a little longer than they might have reasonably expected."

Elizabeth scoffed. "That is ridiculous."

"Perhaps, but one might argue it all the same. Even if it were not the case, I know for certain that your family is much happier seeing you wedded to me rather than that moronic brute. What might he have done to you after you were married? To your mother or one of your sisters after your father's decease?"

Thoughts of Collins always boiled Darcy's blood; how he longed to throttle that sycophantic menace! At least the man had been taught a lesson, however much he deserved a harsher sentence. The village magistrate had written to Darcy to inform him that there was only so much punishment the law was allowed to mete out in a case where no substantial harm was inflicted; however, Collins had suffered much pain and humiliation by being whipped before the entire town. After that, he had been set free and taken himself off to parts unknown. He would still inherit Longbourn one day, but Elizabeth and all the Bennets were now protected from whatever malicious revenge he might concoct, regardless of the length of Mr Bennet's life. Darcy would ensure it. Not that Collins would have much opportunity to act, now that he had to contend with Lady Catherine's wrath.

Perhaps sensing from his tone or posture how overcome he was by resentment of Collins, Elizabeth placed her palm against Darcy's cheek and drew him closer for a soft kiss. When she withdrew, she soothed, "You are correct, of course, but it is over with now. He can no longer hurt any of us, thanks to you."

"I believe you deserve some of the credit, as I have already said."

Elizabeth laughed softly at his persistence and kissed him again. "Very well, I concede the point, but I still cannot help being a bit uneasy about our upcoming visit. Even if my family has forgiven me—and, yes, I am sure that they have—I do worry about how you will react to them. My mother, especially, can be very…excitable, to say nothing of the youngest girls and their lack of restraint. Kitty and Lydia mean no harm, but I know you do not like their wildness."

Darcy pulled Elizabeth into his arms for an embrace. "I promise that I shall exercise the utmost patience with them, if only because you love them so dearly. Your devotion speaks well of them. If they have any measure of your love and esteem, then they shall have mine, also."

"The Gardiners, as well?"

"Of course."

"I really do believe you will like them. They are intelligent, genteel people whom I greatly admire and respect."

Darcy still somewhat doubted this, given Mr Gardiner's close relationship with Mrs Bennet, but supposed he must accept Elizabeth's commendation at face value. If she loved them, then they must deserve it.

"Come, my love," he entreated, ready to abandon their worries for a more agreeable occupation. "Now that I am free from my officious cousins' schemes, let us adjourn to the library for a game of chess, or perhaps a stroll through the orangery."

Elizabeth slipped out of Darcy's hold and issued him a saucy little smile. "Certainly, dearest, but first I must retrieve something from my bedchamber. Might you lend me your assistance?"

Her expression sent Darcy's heart aflutter. In the weeks

since their marriage—before, actually—he had come to understand the meaning of *that* particular look. He needed no flimsy pretext to convince him and swept her out of the saloon and up the stairs with alacrity, Elizabeth giggling at his haste the entire way.

CHAPTER TWENTY-NINE

At the start of February, after bidding Pemberley a fond farewell, the three Darcys piled back into their much abused carriage and travelled the comparatively easy distance to Hertfordshire. There were no mishaps along the road, no delays caused by either God or man, and they arrived at Longbourn in good time. For Elizabeth, who had mixed emotions about the reunion with her family, the journey was almost too efficient for her liking.

As they trundled up Longbourn's drive, Darcy took her hand and squeezed it gently. "All will be well, my love."

Elizabeth ceased the nervous tapping of her foot and returned his reassuring smile with a weak one of her own. She wanted to believe him, but she could not help being a touch anxious.

"Oh, what a charming home!" Georgiana exclaimed, either ignorant of Elizabeth's distress or pretending to be so. "'Tis exactly how I pictured it from your description. I imagine the gardens are absolutely lovely in the summer."

Elizabeth felt a sudden surge of fondness for her new family, both of whom were making a concerted effort to cheer her out of her disquiet. She had made a fortunate alliance, indeed.

The carriage halted in the circular drive, and the Bennets and Mr Bingley spilled from the house. As Darcy handed her down, Elizabeth noted that her mother was fluttering her handkerchief in her usual nervous fashion. Tears pricked at the corners of her eyes. *How I have missed them!*

Evidently, they had missed her as well, for the moment she was on solid ground, her sisters and mother swarmed about her, pulling her into their arms, exclaiming over her new gown, playfully professing themselves envious of her handsome new husband, and insisting on knowing his favourite dish so that it might be served tomorrow.

Mrs Bennet bustled them inside for refreshments, but before Elizabeth could be swept up in the procession, she halted and looked over her shoulder. There was her father, with a familiar twinkle in his eyes. She felt like a small child again as he approached, smiling in that soft, affectionate way he reserved for her. How many times had she seen that same expression upon his whiskery face whilst he read to her from one of his books?

"Welcome home, Lizzy." He corrected himself a moment later. "I suppose this is your home no longer, but you are welcome all the same. Tell me, my girl, is my new son treating you as he should? Shall I be forced to take him to task?"

Sniffling even as she laughed, Elizabeth embraced her father as the last of her worries drifted away.

———— ⋯⚜⋯ ————

ONCE TEA AND CAKE HAD BEEN LIBERALLY PARCELLED OUT TO the gathered crowd and the particulars of the wedding had been discussed—as well as stern reminders to the younger girls to keep to the accepted version of events—conversation turned to apprising Elizabeth of the latest news.

"You and Jane might have got yourselves husbands, Lizzy, but now that the militia are off to Brighton in the spring, there will be no men left for the rest of us!" moaned Lydia with a theatrical air. "Our hearts are broken!"

"Broken!" echoed Kitty with a wail.

"If only Papa would consent to let me travel with Mrs Forster—she is my particular friend, by the by—I should be very well pleased, but he swears he will not." Lydia crossed her arms and glared at their father from across the room. Mr Bennet, apparently sensing his youngest's ire, turned from his conversation with Bingley and raised his teacup in salute. The smile upon his face pronounced him cheerfully unbothered by Lydia's petulance.

"Ha, ha!" Kitty jeered at Lydia, proving exactly why they ought not be allowed out in Meryton by themselves, much less Brighton.

"You are just jealous—"

"Girls, girls! Cease your bickering," interrupted Mrs Bennet with a snap of her fan. "We are to visit Pemberley this summer, which is far superior to anything Brighton has to offer."

For Elizabeth's part, the news of the militia's decampment brought much relief; Mr Wickham would soon be gone and her sisters protected from his villainy. She had not wanted to burden her father with the knowledge of Mr Wickham's proposition when it had occurred, and warning her sisters to stay away from him had resulted in little more than exasperated sighs and much peevishness. Thankfully, Mr Bennet's imposed seclusion had kept them away from the regiment during Elizabeth's unexpected journey.

Once the squabble was quashed, Lydia again turned to Elizabeth. "Losing the militia is cruelty itself, but that is not the worst news. You remember Mr Wickham, do you not?" She punctuated her coy enquiry with a suggestive wiggle of her eyebrows.

Beside her on the sofa, Elizabeth felt Darcy stiffen. She wished she could offer the poor man some relief, but such an endeavour was impossible with her family all gathered. Georgiana, thankfully, had adjourned to the music room with Mary some half an hour ago and was not present to hear any tidings that would pain her. "I do, but I cannot say I have thought of him much since I saw him last."

"Well, he is now engaged to Mary King! I can hardly believe it. Why he should care three straws for her, I shall never know. Have you seen her freckles? Ghastly!"

Again, Kitty mimicked her younger sister's thoughts,

adding, "I am sure he would be in love with *me* if *my* uncle were to leave me ten thousand pounds."

Elizabeth could not disagree with her on that point. She would speak to Darcy about informing Mr King of Mr Wickham's proclivities before they left the area, in the hopes of saving the poor girl and her inheritance from the scoundrel's clutches.

It was time for a change of subject. Turning to Mrs Bennet, she asked, "Have you seen many of our other friends since I have been away?"

"Oh, yes! Ever since Mr Bennet has allowed us out of the house again—not that I agree such seclusion was necessary, mind—we have been all about the neighbourhood spreading our good news! *Two* daughters married, and to such fine gentlemen! Lady Lucas was beside herself with envy." The fact that Jane was, as yet, not quite married seemed to escape Mrs Bennet and provided Elizabeth with much amusement. Jane herself shook her head and sighed, leading Elizabeth to disguise her laugh with a well-placed cough.

After expounding upon this topic for some time to Elizabeth, who listened patiently and nodded when appropriate, Mrs Bennet asserted in a loud whisper, "No one has so much as questioned our story, Lizzy. Why should they? Naturally, a great man such as Mr Darcy would wish to be married from London where his elevated relations might attend him. Why, he cannot be expected to marry in a family parish!" She followed this with an obvious wink, which made her daughter's lips twitch in amusement.

"You are excessively clever, Mama. Tell me, does no one enquire after Mr Collins? The banns had been read, after all."

Mrs Bennet flicked her hand dismissively. "Who cares for Mr Collins? No one! When Mrs Long tried to insinuate that he was misused, I reminded her that Longbourn is nothing to Pemberley, and she had nothing to say to that! Really, who could possibly choose a Mr Collins over a Mr Darcy?"

Elizabeth smirked against the rim of her teacup. "Who, indeed?"

THE DARCYS AGREED TO STAY AT NETHERFIELD. BINGLEY HAD insisted, and Elizabeth was grateful for the offer. She honestly did not wish to tax her husband unduly with too much exposure to her mother and youngest sisters. Bingley's elderly aunt was to act as hostess until Jane could fill the role, which would almost certainly be an improvement on Netherfield's previous mistress. Elizabeth suspected—and Jane heavily implied—that Mrs Bennet's nerves had also been taken into consideration. The wedding was scheduled for the morrow, and it was no great surprise to anyone that Mrs Bennet was suffering from more frequent fits over the myriad extravagant details apparently required to impress Bingley's wealthy, exalted friends. There had been no such fuss over the breakfast for the comparatively inconsequential Mr Collins, but then again, no one was in a celebratory mood save the bridegroom. It occurred to Elizabeth that one benefit of eloping was that she had avoided this fretful whirlwind. Darcy and her father had both snorted into their wine glasses when she had made this observation.

When the time came, after the evening meal, to depart Longbourn for Netherfield, the goodbyes were noisy and plaintive, despite the knowledge that they would all see one another again early the following morning. Elizabeth could not help shedding her share of tears, especially when it came time to say goodnight to Jane. After kissing her sister tenderly on the cheek, Elizabeth congratulated her in a warbling voice. "I am so happy for you, dearest. Mr Bingley will make an excellent husband."

Jane, swiping away moisture from her own cheek, heartily agreed. "We intend to be the happiest couple in the world! Though, perhaps, we have some competition."

Both ladies glanced at Darcy, who was politely suffering the affectionate effusions of Mrs Bennet. Elizabeth experienced another surge of fondness for him at the forbearance he was showing her excitable mother. "Let us agree that we are both exceptionally fortunate. On that score, I want to thank you."

"Thank me? For what?"

"For persuading me to go with Mr Darcy. Were it not for you, I might be Mrs Collins now, miserably pining away in Kent for a life I would never have had. Instead, I am married to the most wonderful man in the world and happier than I deserve."

"Oh, Lizzy," Jane scolded half-heartedly, though she laughed, too. "You are deserving of every good thing."

"Perhaps not so deserving as you, but I shall not quibble over it."

Elizabeth, still gazing adoringly at her husband, caught the very moment Darcy's patience with Mrs Bennet expired. He shot her a beseeching look and she, after trading an amused glance with her sister, determined it was time to intervene. "I believe it is my turn to rush to the rescue."

Finis

ACKNOWLEDGMENTS

I would like to offer my deepest, most heartfelt gratitude to everyone and anyone who assisted me in bringing this novel to completion. Firstly, my husband, who did his level best to watch the kids and let me work as often as possible; thank you for keeping them occupied, I know it wasn't easy. Secondly, to Cat Andrews, who gave me thoughtful feedback before I submitted this story to my publishers; I greatly appreciate you taking the time to do so. Thirdly, I owe a particular debt to my editors. The ingenious V Lewis helped me fill in all the plot holes and plant the seeds of something better in their place; truly, her insight was invaluable. Also Becky Sun who was a thorough, meticulous line editor and helped me get my manuscript to the finish line (and exactly on time, too). And to all my readers on A Happy Assembly and Darcy and Lizzy Forums who provided their thoughts, assistance and encouragement throughout the posting of my first draft, as well as understanding patience when I had to put it on a six month hiatus while I recovered from the aftermath of COVID-19. Thank you so much.

A very special thanks goes to Michelle D'Arcy and Michelle Brown David, both of whom donated money to the fundraiser for Ukraine in exchange for a cameo in this book. See if you can spot them!

Finally, I would very much like to thank Quills & Quartos Publishing, as well as Amy D'Orazio and Jan Ashton specifically, for continuing to believe in me and my writing. I am exceedingly grateful to be part of this publishing house and can hardly believe my good fortune most days.

ABOUT THE AUTHOR

Mary Smythe is a homemaker living in South Carolina with a rather useless BA in English collecting dust in a closet somewhere. Mrs Smythe discovered the works of Jane Austen as a teenager thanks to the 1995 BBC *Pride and Prejudice* miniseries featuring Colin Firth and Jennifer Ehle and has since gone on to read everything written by Miss Austen at least once yearly, always wishing that there were more. She has been writing since 2001, but only discovered Jane Austen Fanfiction in the summer of 2018.

ALSO BY MARY SMYTHE

A Faithful Narrative

Dare to Refuse Such a Man

Pride Before a Fall

Welcome Home

MULTI-AUTHOR COLLECTIONS

'Tis the Season

An Inducement into Matrimony